FLOTILLA ATTACK

FLOTILLA ATTACK

by

Duncan Harding

Dales Large Print Books
Long Preston, North Yorkshire,
BD23 4ND, England.

British Library Cataloguing in Publication Data.

Harding, Duncan
    Flotilla attack.

    A catalogue record of this book is
    available from the British Library

    ISBN   1-84262-383-4 pbk

First published in Great Britain in 1976
by Futura Publications Limited

Copyright © Futura Publications Limited 1976

The moral right of the author has been asserted

Published in Large Print 2005 by arrangement with
Eskdale Publishing

Dales Large Print is an imprint of Library Magna Books Ltd.

Printed and bound in Great Britain by
T.J. (International) Ltd., Cornwall, PL28 8RW

'Man, in the battle of our days, is a man who, hardly knowing how to swim, is suddenly thrown into the sea.'

Ardant du Picq.

A BRIEF GLOSSARY

For those who don't like reading footnotes, here are a few of the naval terms, slang and otherwise, used in this book:

Bangers (or snorkers): sausages.
Burn: to smoke a cigarette.
Buzz: rumour.
Chippy: shipwright.
Defaulters: Parade of offenders against King's Regulations.
ER9: Top grade engine-room artificer.
Gash: rubbish or for free.
Gestapo: Naval police.
Green hand: raw recruit.
Heads: latrines.
Hogwash: the sea.
Jimmy-the-One: the First Lieutenant.
Ky: cocoa.
Last Dog: last dog watch; between 6 and 8 pm.
Matelot: sailor.
Neaters: Neat rum.
Nelson's Blood: Issue rum.
No-Badge A.B.: a term of derision.
Oppo: mate.
Ping: the sound made by the Asdic

submarine hunting device.

Pom-pom (Chicago Piano): multiple-
barrel, anti-aircraft gun.

Rattle: on Defaulters.

Sardines (or 'fish'): torpedoes.

Scouse: Liverpudlian.

Sickbay Tiffy: medical attendant.

Snake Pit: out-of-bounds area, usually
red-light district.

Sprog: rookie.

Stripy: long-service man, with three
good-conduct stripes.

Ticklers: hand-rolled cigarettes.

Tiddley: smart.

Tiddley Oggies: Cornish pasties.

Up the line: on leave.

ONE: *THE INITIATION*

'All right, you old bitch, don't you dare let me down now, or I'll have the knickers off you!'

Lieutenant Commander John Lamb,
February 15th 1940.

ONE

'Here the buggers come!' shouted the young lookout above the shrill clamour of the alarm bells. 'Off the port-bow, sir!'

The Stuka dive-bombers came in from the pale northern sun at 250 mph. On the bridge Lamb acted instinctively. He sprang to the telegraphs. Throwing them fore and aft, he gave two urgent rings for 'full speed ahead'. The deck trembled violently beneath his feet as the lean destroyer surged forward. Next to him the pale young coxswain started to zig-zag instinctively, body tensed for the imminent attack.

Down below on the deck, the gun crews were pelting for the pom-poms, slipping on their grey flash gear and helmets as they ran, while the alarm bells rang their urgent warning. The door to the bridge was flung open. Captain Homes stood there, naked save for his gold-braided cap and the white lather of shaving soap around his heavy chin.

'Where are they, Number One?' he demanded.

Lieutenant Lamb did not get a chance to reply.

At that moment, the Stuka leader flung

13

himself out of the sky, hurtling downwards, sirens screaming, engine howling protestingly. To a mesmerised Lamb it seemed that the German pilot must crash into the green heaving sea below.

'Hard to port!' yelled Homes.

The sweating coxswain flung the destroyer round. The Stuka broke out of its dive, air brakes screaming. A myriad deadly black eggs tumbled from its light blue belly, as it soared upwards following the ugly brown puff-balls of the ack-ack. As the destroyer swung to port, the stick of bombs burst a mere hundred yards away, sending up sheets of white and green water higher than their mast. The destroyer trembled like a live thing.

'Get those pom-poms into action!' yelled Lamb from the bridge as the second Stuka came roaring in. There was a rapid throaty punch-punch of the first gun opening up. Angry red-glowing shells curved low across the heaving water. Black pieces of metal were breaking away from the German plane but the pilot pressed home his attack. Thick white glycol began to stream from the Stuka's engine. Lamb could see the plane's black-and-white cross insignia quite clearly now. A wing fell off, fluttering to the sea like a great leaf.

'For Chrissake, knock the bastard out of the sky!' shouted the Captain.

The stricken German plane hit the bows at 300 mph, crumpling them like a banana skin. Lieutenant Lamb hit the deck as the Stuka's bombs exploded in a blinding flash of harsh scarlet flame and the stricken destroyer came to a sudden halt. For a moment the First Officer blacked out.

When he opened his eyes again, HMS *Blackamore* was fighting for her life, a smoking wreck, the water pouring into her crumpled bows by the ton, while her gunners peppered the sky all around, trying in vain to beat off the triumphant Stukas.

'Lamb, get them up from below – *now!*' the Captain roared above the furious chatter of the pom-poms and the hysterical scream of the dive-bombers' sirens.

Lamb shook his head and pulled himself to his feet. The skipper was clinging to the handrail, his right foot poised at an un-natural angle, blood jetting from a lacerated wound below his knee.

'But, skipper!' he protested, 'we've not–'

'No buts, Number One. Get them up. The *Blackamore*'s had it! We'll have to abandon her!'

Lamb pelted down the bridge ladder. The deck was littered with dead and dying sailors. Flames were already beginning to lick greedily at the paintwork. He grabbed hold of the nearest phone. All he could get from the engine room was a confused babble of sound. The men down there might well have been speaking a foreign language for all he understood. He jammed it back on its cradle. At that same moment, the destroyer gave a violent lurch and started to heel to port.

He fought his way into the lower deck, crunching his way across smashed crockery. 'Get up top everybody!' he shouted. 'We're abandoning ship!'

The white-faced stewards and sick-berth attendants needed no urging. They began to file up the ladder. Lamb pushed his way past them to the engine room. The sweating, black-faced stokers in their dirty white overalls were already up to their knees in water, but they had not yet abandoned their posts.

'All right, everybody out!' he roared as the ship heeled and tools showered down from their racks. 'Come on, get a move on! We haven't got all—'

As he spoke the dim green secondary lighting went out and they were in total darkness, every man for himself. 'Don't panic, lads!' the Scots Chief ER9 bellowed, 'remember you're British!'

'Ay,' a thick Yorkshire voice answered, 'but do them bloody Jerries up there know that!'

There was a ripple of laughter, and the stokers scrambled through the chaotic darkness to the upper deck. Lamb made a last check as best he could, wading up to his waist through the icy North Sea water; then he followed, levering himself upwards using feed pumps, pipes, valves – anything that would give him a purchase.

HMS *Blackamore* was leaning over at a forty-five-degree angle, its derrick gear dangling into the oil-heavy swell like a monstrous fishing rod. Lamb fought his way to the bridge. The Captain was dying. It was obvious as he stood there, clutching the rail, the knuckles of his tightly clenched hands white, his naked feet in a pool of blood. Behind him the young coxswain was sobbing softly, the tears running down his smooth cheeks, as he still attempted to steer the sinking ship.

'Well?' the Captain demanded through gritted teeth.

'All out, sir – all who can be got out, sir.'

'Good. Thanks, Number One.' He turned slowly and very stiffly, as if every movement required an extreme effort of will. 'All right, Conway, you can go over the side now... You've done a good job – and stop bloody snivelling.'

'Ay, ay, sir – and thank you, sir.' The coxswain let go of the wheel as if he had suddenly discovered it was red hot. A second later he was gone, pulling his shoes off as he ran to the side.

'What now, sir?' Lamb asked.

'What do you think?'

'How do you mean, sir?'

'I'm staying, Number One.' He stared challengingly at the younger officer.

'But–'

'There are no buts, Number One. Even if you did manage to get me off, this leg of mine would have to come off.' He winced with pain. 'And I don't fancy limping around with a tin pin for the rest of my natural while you young uns get all the glory.'

Lamb swallowed, realising as he spoke what he was committing himself to, and trying to keep his voice calm, 'then I'll stay with you, Captain.'

Captain Homes, no longer looking ridiculous as he leaned there naked, with the shaving soap still clinging to his chin, stared hard at Lamb's harshly handsome young face. 'You're a good officer, Lamb. You've got the makings of an admiral, just like your poor old father–' He winced again, his faded blue eyes liquid with pain. 'The phoney war's over – and the Royal Navy's going to have the need of your like before this show's over. So you're going, Lamb – and that's an order...'

First Lieutenant Lamb hesitated, then clicked to attention and saluted. 'Thank you, sir,' he snapped. 'I shall go, then.'

But Captain Homes was no longer listening, and an instant later Lamb was pelting down the crazily tilted bridge ladder. 'She's going now!' yelled a dozen constricted throats as the men trod water or hung on to the sides of the Carley floats. The muffled explosion was followed by the unholy shriek of rending metal. Flames leapt from the destroyer's aft, colouring the sailors' strained faces blood-red. The mast toppled forward into the crackling torment of sudden fire.

'She's going to turn over!' cried the wizened toothless PO, treading water next to Lamb.

He nodded mutely, as HMS *Blackamore* heeled over like some giant metallic whale. He caught a glimpse of the still spinning discs of the destroyer's phosphor-bronze propellers as the greedy waves rolled forward to claim her. The water beat itself into a frenzy. Lamb knew he should order the survivors to get further away. But he was mesmerised by the sight.

As the boiling tumult of water surged upwards to devour her, it threw a body into the air: a grey-haired, three-striper, a puppet of whirling arms and legs which became in death a figure of burning anger and reproach. For a moment the dead sailor seemed to hang in the grey steaming air, as if cursing all those who had survived to fight the new war.

Then he was gone and the ship too, and a suddenly alert Lieutenant Lamb was

19

shouting frantically: 'Pull away, lads! For God's sake, pull away – before she drags the lot of us down with her.'

TWO

'His Majesty's Ship *Rose*,' Lieutenant Commander Lamb read from the gleaming new brass name plate on the refitted destroyer's quarterdeck.

'Ay,' said the small, brisk shipyard foreman, wearing the traditional badge of his office – a black bowler tilted at a cocky angle, 'it's a right funny name for a fighting ship, I agree.' He swept his knowing gaze along the destroyer's two-hundred-foot, newly painted length. 'But you know, Commander, call a rose by any other name–'

He didn't complete the old cliché. He didn't have to, both of them, civilian and sailor, knew HMS *Rose*'s unfortunate history. She had been designed and built under the Admiralty's Emergency War Programme of 1918, but she had never seen any naval action. Nevertheless, in the two decades of her existence, she had experienced violence enough: beached and virtually wrecked off the Chinese coast in the '20s; nearly scuttled by a mutinous crew during the 1931 'troubles'; and now jinxed by the suicide of her skipper in the Mediterranean.

'Naturally,' the shipyard foreman continued, raising his voice over the clatter of the yard, 'she's pretty slow by Tribal class* standards. But all the same, she'll outgun them with those new five-inchers we've put in her. And after all, we should know, we built both the *Afridi* and the *Cossack.*'

Lieutenant Commander Lamb took his eyes off the ship and told himself that after fourteen years in the Navy he should not be so naïve about the fact that this was his very first command. 'I hope you're right, Mr Smithers. But there's no denying the fact that she's pretty slow by modern destroyer standards. A good five knots behind the Tribals at least.' He smiled, erasing for a moment the hard lines etched in his lean face by the last six months of arduous sea duty in the North Sea in the *Blackamore,* which had won him the DSC but had lost him most of his friends and shipmates. 'Ah well, as long as we've got a good strong wind from behind, I expect we'll be able to keep up. Now then where's all that bumf of yours that I have to sign before I go aboard?'

Together they walked past the line of over-alled workers dragging a huge rusty chain behind them with the easy carelessness of men who knew it was going to be a long war

*At that time, the Royal Navy's most advanced destroyer class, which included the *Cossack* and the *Afridi*.

and didn't see any necessity for haste, and passed into the dock office. The shipyard foreman took off his bowler, hung it up on the Victorian hatstand, rubbed his hands on the sides of his jacket as if to clean them, and then produced the release document.

John Lamb scanned it through. 'We Messrs Leslie & Co Ltd,' he read under his breath, 'Hebburn-on-Tyne at/off the Tyne handed over this fifteenth day of February, 1940 at 2.30 pm o'clock His Majesty's Ship *Rose* to his Majesty's Navy. Received from Messrs. Leslie & Co this date without prejudice to outstanding liabilities.' Slowly he took out his Parker and unscrewed the cap. He bent down, then hesitated.

'Anything wrong, Commander?' the foreman asked anxiously. Leslie's had a long reputation to live up to; they had been building fighting ships since just after Trafalgar.

'No, nothing,' Lamb answered without looking up. He scrawled his signature under the release form. The foreman snatched it up, and opening a drawer, thrust it inside, as if he were afraid that the young officer, with the new ribbon of the DSC on the breast of his sea-faded serge working jacket, might change his mind.

He thrust out his hand. 'I'd like to wish you the best of luck, Commander.'

'Thank you.' Lamb smiled. 'And I'll

probably need it too.'

The foreman smiled back, but his dark eyes did not light up. Anyone going to war in a jinx ship like HMS *Rose* definitely did need luck.

A moment later Lamb passed into the noisy yard alone and strode towards his ship with the barrage balloons tethered above him in the wintry sky like fat grey slugs. At the bottom of the gang plank, he drew a deep breath and hesitated for an instant. At last he was stepping aboard his own ship for the first time in his fourteen-year career. It was a good feeling. He slapped his hand down on the railing.

'All right, you old bitch,' he whispered under his breath, 'don't you dare let me down now, or I'll have the knickers off you!' Then he was taking the rungs two at a time.

Lieutenant James Pollacks, RN, known as 'Jimmy Ballocks' behind his back, marched smartly across the littered deck towards the new skipper, his skinny chest thrust out and his weak jaw jutting upwards, as if he owned every rivet of the *Rose*. Behind him, Petty Officer Degenhardt followed at a respectful distance, but his hard face could not quite conceal the look of contempt it always bore when he was in the presence of the *Rose*'s First Officer.

At the regulation six paces Pollacks came

to a halt and swung Lamb an immaculate salute. 'Welcome aboard, sir. I'm Pollacks, sir, your new Number One.' He thrust out a gloved hand without turning his head. 'Petty Officer Degenhardt, sir. The coxswain.'

'*Sir!*' the PO barked in a harsh voice, as if he were back at the depot.

Lamb looked at the PO's lined face, dominated by a flat mis-shapen nose. The accent was as German as the name.

He returned the men's salutes and stretched out his hand. 'I hear you are the only two of the original crew still aboard, Number One?'

Pollacks fumbled with his fancy glove. 'We're the *only* two aboard until the draft arrives, sir.' Pollacks hand was soft and slightly damp.

'I see. Where is the draft coming from?'

'We've got fifty of the original crew from the Med. You know that business with the late skipper had its effect. Sailors are suspicious creatures. They–'

Lamb cut him short with a quick wave of his hand, somehow taking an instinctive dislike to his new First Officer. 'And where are the rest coming from?'

'From the depots, sir. HO men* for the most part, as far as I can make out.'

Lamb pursed his lips. Not only would he

*Hostilities Only (ie wartime service only).

be in charge of one of the slowest destroyers in the fleet, but his crew would be made up of mainly rookies. It wasn't exactly a good start to his new command. Still, he told himself, it was better than no command. 'All right, Number One, let me see the officers as they come aboard and one hour after the draft arrives, parade them down here and I'll talk to them.'

'But you know the wartime trains, sir,' Pollacks protested. 'They might come straggling in at all hours.'

'You're probably right, Number One,' Lamb said easily. 'But from now onwards, I'll see every new man within an hour of his arrival on the ship. Got it?'

'Got it, sir,' Pollacks answered without enthusiasm.

Behind him, Degenhardt's battered face relaxed into a slow smile for the first time that day. Lamb smiled too. Somehow he felt he had found an ally, German or no German.

Two hours later the draft arrived and Petty Officer Degenhardt ordered 'clear lower deck' to be piped. Slowly and a little grumpily the new arrivals, stiff and dirty from the long train journey from the south, began to form up under the Coxswain's hard Prussian gaze.

A handful of them were veterans, still

wearing the white caps of the *Rose*'s last commission in the Med, their faces bronzed, their uniforms worn, and their kitbags stiff with deep sea salt and bleached by the suns of Africa. Others were older men, obviously misfits and trouble-makers, eagerly transferred by grateful captains, happy to be rid of them. Spivs, they called them in the Navy, dressed in skin-tight 'tiddly suits',★ with enormous bell bottoms and with the sleeves of their jumpers rolled back to display the full glory of their cheap chromium wrist watches. Shoulders slightly hunched, as if they expected to have to ward off a blow at any moment, their faces were set in a permanent look of sour disgust.

But most of the draft were 'green hands', pale-faced callow youngsters, called up at the beginning of the war and rushed through the three month training course in the Southern depots. Most of them, Degenhardt told himself, as they shuffled into three sloppy ranks, would probably spend their first week, at sea lying in their 'pits' groaning and spewing up their cookies.

'All right,' he barked when they had finally settled down, 'pay attention to me you lot, before the Captain comes. I'm Degenhardt – Petty Officer Degenhardt, the *Rose*'s

★Seaman's slang for his Number One uniform.

Coxswain.' He paused and swept his gimlet-like gaze along their ranks.

'Great balls of fire,' Scouse MacFadden whispered out of the corner of his mouth to his 'oppo' 'Bunts', otherwise known as Leading Signaller Smith, 'did we catch the wrong train – and join the sodding German Navy?'

Degenhardt's face tensed. In the last eight years since he had fled Germany after that fatal run-in with the SA man, he had heard comments like that often enough.

'All right, I heard that,' he snapped. 'And you're right. I'm a Jerry, a Hun, a Square-Head or I was till King George decided to honour me with British citizenship, for what that's worth,' he smiled, showing a mouthful of small, sharp yellow teeth. 'So that makes me a double bastard, don't it – Jerry and Coxswain, as well!' The smile vanished as suddenly as it had come, as if his jaw were worked by a steel spring. His eyes blazed abruptly, twin fires of hate, which, whether they were genuine or not, frightened the life out of the suddenly attentive green hands. 'Now then, I hope we understand each other. Because anyone of your shower who sets a foot wrong, is going to be in for trouble – real trouble – with Petty Officer Horst Degenhardt. *Got it?*'

Behind him the Coxswain heard the two officers approaching across the deck. Without looking round, he drew a deep breath and bellowed; 'Ship's company – ship's company, *attention!*'

The draft came to attention sloppily and stared at the young officer in the faded uniform with his cap set at the rakish angle affected by destroyer skippers. In his turn, Lamb stared back for a moment and was not impressed by what he saw. Then he forced a slight smile and stood them at ease.

He began his little speech of welcome without hesitation; he had heard the late Captain Homes give it often enough in the past to new drafts. Yet now, he uttered the old clichés with real conviction, 'You see,' he concluded, 'it's been my experience that you can't have a happy ship unless you have an efficient one. That is the way I intend to start this new commission – with an efficient *and* a happy ship.' He paused and stared along their apathetic ranks; at that moment the draft looked both unhappy and inefficient. 'Now, then, the Admiralty usually allows a captain three weeks to work up a newly refitted ship. I have decided we'll do the job in three days!'

There was a gasp of surprise from the crew. He had expected and was pleased with the reaction; at least he had shaken them out of their sullen complacency.

He smiled. 'I'm glad the news pleases you. But to soften the blow, you'll have the rest of the day to yourselves after the Coxswain dismisses you. Remember though, I want every man back on board by zero twenty-three hundred. We start the working-up at first light.' He swung round to Degenhardt, whose dark eyes reflected a certain restrained admiration for the way the new skipper had handled the draft. 'All right, Coxswain,' he said, 'they're all yours now.' And in a quick whisper, he added, 'and give 'em hell from tomorrow onwards!'

Just as the winter dusk was settling down over the Yard and the weary workers were beginning to knock off for the day, Pollacks announced the arrival of the deck officers. 'Three of them, all subs and still wet behind the ears,' he said almost gleefully. 'Couldn't fight their way out of a paper bag – a wet one – by the looks of them.'

'I see,' Lamb said coldly.

Pollacks did not appear to notice the snub. 'I wonder if I could go ashore for a couple of hours, skipper? You see, I've got a hot little number waiting for me in the Station Hotel in Newcastle.' He winked knowingly. 'And one's got to keep the homes fires – er – burning, hasn't one?'

'One has,' Lamb answered, ignoring the chummy wink. 'Yes, off you go, Number One. I'll see the subs alone.'

The three Sub-Lieutenants were very

smart in their number one uniforms, looking as if they had just stepped out of the illustrated section of the Manual of Training. Obviously they were all three straight from *King Alfred*, though the taller of the three, who wore the 'Canada' patch on his shoulder, was at least a half a dozen years older than the other two.

Lamb glanced swiftly through the folders they had brought with them and gave them the same little talk that Captain Homes had given him when he had joined HMS *Blackamore* as a Sub in 1936, before allotting Ferris, the short, fair, spotty one, to the Signals. 'And remember,' he warned him, 'those sparks and bunts are the smartest matelots aboard. They'll take a rise out of you unless you can read and send quicker than they can. So you'll have to get your finger out very niftily over the next few weeks. Clear?'

'Clear, sir.'

Lamb turned to the next sub, a thin, dark-haired Welsh officer named Gowan, who had been studying engineering at Cambridge when he had volunteered for the Royal Naval Voluntary Reserve. 'All right, Gowan, you've got the artillery. With your background, I think you're best fitted for that particular job.'

'Thank you, sir.'

'Don't thank me, Sub,' Lamb grinned.

'Wait till you hear what your men call you.'

'Sir?'

'If you're lucky, the Welsh Wizard. If you're unlucky – Gowan the Guns.

'All right the two of you, cut along while I deal with – er – Doan here. I'll see you both in the wardroom for a drink in thirty minutes' time.'

'All right, Doan,' Lamb said after the other two had gone. 'You're the oldest and you seem to have gained excellent marks in navigation at HMS *King Alfred,* so I want to have you with me on the bridge.'

The Canadian smiled lazily. 'Sure, skipper,' he answered, 'it would suit me just fine.'

Lamb looked up at Doan curiously. 'Your record states,' he said after a moment, 'that you enlisted in Kingston, Ontario, two days after the war had broken out and that after three months of sea duty, you asked for and were transferred to the UK for commission training because – according to your own words – "that's where the action is".' Lamb pursed his lips, wondering for an instant how he should pose his next question. 'But frankly, Doan, you don't sound like any Canuck I've ever heard.'

'Well, sir, I'm really what you might call a latterday Empire Loyalist from Annapolis who emigrated to Canada a couple of hundred years later.'

'You mean you were US Navy?'

'Right in one, sir. Lootenant – excuse me, *Left*enant, Junior Grade, destroyers.'

'What! But why? The US isn't at war with Germany!'

'I know, sir. But your war, phoney as it may be, is the only war around and it was better than being a fancy pant Admiral's aide in Washington, which I was before I decided to – er – leave the US service.'

Lamb stared up at his lazy face incredulously. 'You mean,' he stuttered, 'that you deserted to join the Canadian Navy?'

'Well, skipper, if you like to put it that crudely, yeah.'

Lamb gave a mock groan and clapped his hand to his forehead. 'What a crew! A draft of green hands and misfits from the depots, a Prussian petty officer as my coxswain, most of my officers straight from *King Alfred* – and now my navigating officer turns out to be a deserter from the US Navy, God preserve me!'

Doan grinned. 'It all goes to make up for a happy ship, sir! And do I get to have a drink in the wardroom too, sir?'

Lamb grabbed his cap. 'You do, Doan. And I'm gong to have one with you. A nice big double pink gin – I need it after this day.' He smiled. 'Glad to have you aboard, Doan. A volunteer and experienced to boot, Doan, you're worth your weight in pink gins on old HMS *Rose*...'

Tired as he was after a long day and feeling the effect of two double pink gins on an empty stomach, Lieutenant Commander John Lamb had one more duty to complete before he turned in for the night. He had to write to his mother. Thus as the yard settled down for the night, its silence broken only by the measured tread of the naval sentries and the drunken singing of some matelot staggering home from a dockside pub, he began the task in the hot tight little cabin, which had now acquired the grand title of the 'Captain's Quarters' on the letterhead.

'Dear Mother,' he wrote. 'I know you will have been worried not to have heard from me since I wrote to you about the gong and the promotion. I hope, however, I didn't worry you too much. You see I wanted to make one hundred per cent certain before I told you – *I've been given my own ship!*' Carefully he underlined the words with the aid of his sliderule.

'I can't give you her name for the time being. All I can say is that she's rather long in the tooth, seen more service than she should have done, has had a bit of damned bad luck in the past and she'll probably be regarded as something of a slow coach by the others when she comes – God willing – to join a flotilla. But still she's *all* mine! That's what counts, isn't it?

'But please understand. I'm not only awfully pleased for myself, but also for you, Mother, and above all for Father. It shows that the sealords have probably forgotten the past and have confidence in the Lamb family again. And believe me, I shall live up to that confidence too, if only for Dad's sake.'

Lamb put down his pen for a moment. Outside, the drunken matelot was singing in a coarse slurred voice, 'and the mate at the wheel had a bloody good feel at the girl I left behind me'. Lamb did not hear the words of the song. His mind was full of that terrible day when they had found his father, dead in his study overlooking the Sound, his old service revolver in his right hand, the shattered photograph of himself, bearded and with the stiff wing collar of the old Navy, in the other. His mother had not cried then, nor had she cried when the *Times* had refused his obituary notice and not a single old comrade or shipmate had turned up for the funeral in the village church's un-hallowed ground. It had taken her a whole year before she had broken down and sobbed as if she would never stop again. That was when John Lamb had announced he was going to ask his prep school head to recommend him for Dartmouth.

But that was the past, he told himself as he picked up his pen again, over fourteen years ago. Now, despite the prejudice he had encountered from the very first day at Dartmouth when his fellow cadets had jeered at him and thrown him in the swimming pool, he had made it. The son of the Royal Navy's most celebrated coward of the 20th century had been given his first command. 'So you see, Mother,' he concluded, 'it won't be an easy command. But I am determined to do my best and I know, despite all her defects, my ship is going to be OK.'

THREE

The dock-hands of the first morning shift gave her a weary cheer as she drew away on the start of her three day working-up exercises; and as HMS *Rose* passed slowly down the river, both merchant and naval vessels lining the stream hastened her on her way with short sharp bursts on their sirens.

'A nice gesture, Number One,' Doan commented happily, looking up from his charts.

Pollacks, his head still heavy from the night before, and in a black mood, grunted sourly: 'Probably glad to see the back of us more likely. Now keep your mind on your business, will you?'

'Ay, ay, sir,' Doan answered cheerfully, and under his breath recommended the Lieutenant to carry out a fairly impossible sexual act with himself.

Slowly the destroyer passed Tyne Dock, the Jarrow Staithes, the Pilot House and the Black Middens, the terror of even the most experienced of Tyne river pilots. But the ugly black rocks to port presented no problem to Doan, who skirted them as though he had been negotiating the fast-running river all his life.

The *Rose* began to pick up speed. Within the hour, nearly a quarter of the new crew were lying in their hammocks, their faces green, the sweat standing out in opaque pearls on their foreheads, groaning miserably and spilling their 'cookies', just as PO Degenhardt had confidently predicted the day before.

But Captain Lamb was in no mood to be merciful. He ordered Degenhardt to rouse them out. 'They can be seasick on their own time, not on the Navy's, Coxswain. Get them back on duty. They might as well start getting used to this.'

Lamb was here, there and everywhere as he ran the *Rose* through her steering trials, log trials, direction-finding trials, checking everything, seeing everything, criticising everything.

Before the midday meal it was the engine room: they were too slow giving him full power; they didn't react quickly enough to the steering orders from the bridge, and failed to get the maximum power out of their engines when he ordered the ship manoeuvred on one boiler. As the sweating, crimson-faced Scots ER9 complained bitterly to anyone who was prepared to listen, 'What does yon man expect from an engine room that's twenty years out of date and manned by a bunch of civvie layabouts – *a bluidy miracle?*'

But that was exactly what it seemed as if Captain Lamb did expect, when he turned his attention to the deck in the afternoon. He caught the crew and their officers on the hop when he ordered everyone to change roles: signallers would have a go at manning the five-inchers, seamen were to take over the tricky task of hoisting the flag signals, while the gunners were suddenly ordered to remove their helmets and flash-gear and commence normal routine deck duties.

The result was chaos, saved only from a complete breakdown by the efforts of the deck officers, who suddenly found themselves sweating and cursing in their shirt-sleeves at the side of the confused crew, trying to cover up the worst faults of the inexperienced sailors as best they could.

'My God, Doan,' Pollacks cursed to the grinning American, as the two of them tried to remove a five-inch shell which had become jammed in A-turret before the Captain spotted yet another failure, 'what kind of skipper is he? He'll be asking his officers to clean out the ruddy heads* next!'

Doan wiped the sweat off his red face with a grease-stained arm and nodded sagely. 'Yeah, Number One, I think that's on the schedule for tomorrow morning.'

*The latrines.

By nightfall, Lamb knew the worst. His engine room was inefficient; despite all the efforts of the long-service ER9 in charge, his junior officers, with the exception of Doan, were completely inept. His crew would panic if the *Rose* ever had to function under action conditions, and worst of all, his First Officer Pollacks was a moaner and a shirker who could not be relied upon to support him in a crisis.

Just after the ship had blacked out for the night, he called PO Degenhardt to his cabin and told him to sit down on the only other chair in the place. 'Coxswain,' he said carefully, 'I want to ask you a question and I want you to give me an honest answer. What do they look like to you?'

Degenhardt looked across at him cautiously, his face hollowed out by the glare of the desk light. 'What do you mean, sir, exactly?'

'I mean the crew. How are they bearing up?'

'Not very well. It's been a hard day for the young ones, and naturally the skivvers haven't helped much, sir. Down below the sea-lawyers are working on the sprogs.* It's only to be expected.' He shrugged. 'Half the supper went overboard – they were too sick or tired to eat it. And most of them didn't

*Young rookies.

40

even want their issue rum.'

Lamb gave him a little smile. 'They must have been in a bad way if they didn't want their Nelson's blood, Coxswain. All the same we can't let up. If they train hard, the real thing won't be so difficult for them. I don't know who said it, but isn't there a saying – train hard, fight soft?'

'I don't know about that, sir,' Degenhardt answered. 'But in the old Imperial Navy, we used to say *marschieren oder kreprieren* – march or croak.'

Lamb looked at him in surprise. 'You mean you were in the German Navy before 1918?'

Degenhardt gave him a crooked smile. 'That's right, sir. I was at the Skar – the Battle of Jutland, as you call it.'

'Good grief, Coxswain, my father fought there... But we can't go into that. Now listen, I want you to go to the wardroom and ask for Mr Doan. I've already spoken to him. He'll give you a hand. Then go up to that target on the aft deck and this is what you'll do...'

'Scouse' MacFadden had had the last dog watch on the floorplates and now he leaned against the gun-shield of 'A' gun, sipping steaming-hot 'ky' and listening to the chatter of some of the old crew, before he slung his hammock for the rest of the night.

As usual they were complaining, nothing new in His Majesty's ships, he knew, but on this particular ship it seemed the crew did little else. Idly he listened to their low-pitched voices as they outdid each other in their griping.

'She's not a happy ship, I tell yer, mon,' one of them was saying in a thick Scots accent. 'She had a jinx on her in the China Sea in the old days. She had a jinx on her in the Med last year. And now she's got a sodding captain who's got a jinx on him from the start.'

'What do yer mean, mate?' queried a Cockney voice.

'Well you know what his old man did in the last do, don't yer?'

The speaker cleared his throat importantly, as if he were about to launch into a long and exciting explanation. But just then the alarm bells shrilled from below, setting in motion a wild burst of frantic movement the length and breadth of ship which quickly filtered to the darkened deck. Half-naked men ran towards their stations, blundering and crashing into each other in the darkness, cursing wildly as they did so.

'Oh my Christ,' Scouse swore to himself as he doubled to his gun, his cup crashing to the deck, 'here we bloody well go again!'

Five minutes later the various deck crews were closed up, and Scouse and the rest of his crew in A-turret learned to their disgust that it wasn't the real thing; the Captain had simply sounded 'action stations' for a practice night shoot at a target which the Coxswain and Mr Doan had thrown overboard thirty minutes before. 'Would you believe it,' the young gun-layer complained. 'After a day like that – and he calls out the whole ship at this time of night. The man's real bloody-minded!'

But there was no time for further complaints. Already the ranges were being shouted down from the bridge and Gowan the Guns was dashing from turret to turret anxiously, cursing to himself in Welsh as he checked that everything was all right. Swiftly they closed on the target as they sped across the dark water with the silver clouds scudding above them. 'Four thousand ... three thousand five hundred ... three thousand...'

'Target bearing ... red four five,' Sub-Lieutenant Doan bellowed from the bridge, 'range three thousand ... *open fire!*'

Scouse, as leading hand, waited anxiously while the young gun-layer found the target. '*On!*' he yelled from where he crouched over the sight and Scouse knew from the tone of his voice that this was his first night shoot.

Scouse sucked in a deep breath and bellowed, '*Shoot!*'

The 5-inch guns erupted violently. A burst

of scarlet flame and acrid yellow smoke blinded him. Automatically he opened his mouth to prevent his eardrums from being burst by the blast which struck him in the face. Then he cursed violently. The young gun-layer had panicked. He had fired on the forward roll of the waves so that the guns had been pointing downwards.

'You silly bleeding pregnant penguin of a sprog!' he yelled at the gun-layer, 'you haven't got the sense you was soddingly well born with! Now get on that damn target. That first shot wouldn't even have frightened a ruddy rowing boat!'

In his haste to make up for the mistake, Scouse forgot an elementary safety precaution; he got too close to one of the breeches. As a result when the guns fired again, the breech sliding back in a cloud of smoke caught him directly in the pit of the stomach. He went down immediately, right on to his knees on the littered gun deck, his face contorted with agony.

'*Scouse!*' the gun-layer yelled in alarm. Next to the kneeling man, a scared-looking young rating rushed forward to help him, but Scouse warded him off with an angry wave of his hand. 'Get off me, yer silly bugger... Get back to your post!'

Clutching one hand to his injured stomach, he staggered to his feet groggily. Through teeth gritted with pain, he cried: 'Now I

44

didn't see where that bugger went. But the next one better hit the target, or me and the Skipper is gonna have the knackers off'n you, mate... Now prepare to shoot!'

Leaning over the bridge railing and watching the events in A-turret, Captain Lamb's handsome face relaxed a little. For the first time on that long miserable day, he felt the stirrings of hope.

On the afternoon of the third and final day of the ship's working-up exercises as Doan was working out a course for the Tyne, the *Rose* was struck by one of those sudden storms for which that part of the North Sea was infamous in winter. One minute the sea was its usual stretch of swaying sea-green monotony, the next the glass was falling and mountainous waves were pounding the ship's beam. The destroyer rolled, at the mercy of the sudden gale, the water striking her with solid blows that sent a shudder through every plate and buried her stern in cascades of white foam. For a moment she would balance on the peak of each breaker, her screws clean out of the water raging below, before falling with a suddenness that sent the pots and pans rattling crazily in the galleys and those of the green hands not on duty vomiting where they lay.

Hour after hour, as the little grey ship, dwarfed into insignificance by the frightening power and majesty of the storm, fought its way back to the mouth of the Tyne. By nightfall the tempest had reached its full fury and the estuary was still nowhere in sight. The wind howled all around them, whipping the sea into a vivid-grey, white-flecked enemy, showering the decks with a vicious icy spray and smashing tons of solid water against the bridge.

The night passed in black, terrifying misery, which had even the normally calm Doan muttering anxiously to himself, as he hunched over his swaying charts in the corner of the bridge. 'I don't believe it... I just don't believe it!' But as the smudged white of the false dawn glimmered on the horizon to the West, the storm finally began to abate, and the howling wind which had deafened them all the previous day finally dropped, leaving behind it a strangely echoing silence. Doan dropped off into an uneasy doze and Lamb did not attempt to waken him. The American deserter had worked hard during the last three days and besides Lamb wanted to be alone with his own thoughts for a while until they reached the mouth of the Tyne.

He knew that he would have to carry the crew – or at least most of them. The last three days had proved that. He would have to control and check everything, to drive the men and himself mercilessly, if he didn't want to fail. For him there could be no fixed watch, no time off, no few precious hours when he might sleep or relax while they were at sea. Grimly he stared at the beige wash of the dawn sky, his hands clenching the bridge rail aggressively until the knuckles whitened with the pressure.

'Sir.'

A voice broke into his reverie. It was the German Coxswain, two steaming hot mugs clasped in his big fists, both adorned with the old legend 'PIYD', which he knew meant 'pinch if you dare'.

'For you and Mr Doan, sir. Coffee au bromide, as the matelots call it.' Degenhardt's battered face relaxed momentarily, 'and I've banged a tot of rum in both of them, sir.'

Lamb accepted the half-pint, chipped tin mug gratefully. 'Just what the doctor ordered, Coxswain – thank you,' he said, touched. 'But let Mr Doan sleep a little while longer. He's beat.'

'They all are, sir,' Degenhardt said hesitantly, but encouraged by the slight smile on the Captain's face as he sipped the burning hot drink. 'It's been a rough three days for most of them.'

Lamb nodded understandingly. 'Do you think I'm working them too hard, Coxswain? After all, it'll probably be weeks before they allot us to an active service flotilla.'

Degenhardt shook his head firmly. 'No sir,

47

not one bit of it. I know my country – er – the Germans. They won't sit on their backsides in Kiel and Wilhelmshaven like they did in the last war.'

Lamb lowered his mug and looked at the Coxswain curiously. For a fleeting second, he wondered how it must feel to know that one day you would have to fight against the men you had once served with. 'How do you mean, Coxswain?' he asked.

'The old Admirals have long gone, sir. Except perhaps for Raeder, the young ones are different. They're Hitler's men and they believe in attack like he does. Believe me, sir, the old *Rose* will be going into action soon enough.'

FOUR

Action came sooner than Petty Officer Horst Degenhardt had anticipated. Just as the look-out spotted the first grey smudge of the North-East Coast, 'Bunts' Smith, the Scouse's friend, clattered up the steps to the bridge, excitedly bearing an urgent signal. It read: *'Tanker in trouble position 055 degrees 05 minutes north, 001 degrees 07 minutes west. Minelaying U-boat in the vicinity. Proceed to area and intercept.'*

In a flash, the whole ship was alarmed. With the bells screaming their stomach-churning call to 'action stations', and the deck full of half-naked, cursing, sliding seamen hurrying frantically into their gear as they ran to their posts across the slick metal plates, HMS *Rose* picked up speed, the Scots ER9 giving her all his 30,000 HP engines could produce.

The bridge was crowded with the three deck officers, Lamb, Doan and Pollacks, anxiously searching the horizon for the tanker, and more important, the mine-laying sub which they reasoned had been the cause of her 'trouble'.

They spotted the tanker first, well down at

the stern, a plume of oil-tinged smoke rising two hundred feet into the sullen morning sky, flames crawling rapidly up her crazily slanted deck, driving the survivors relentlessly backwards to the bows and the water beyond.

They came closer and closer, hearing the mournful tolling of some bell – later they learned it was the Groyne fog bell – which seemed to be sounding the death knell of the men trapped on the tanker. Then they could smell the sickening odour of diesel oil and hear the men's panic stricken cries for help as they sighted the destroyer. Here and there a seaman, crazed with fear by the greedy flames, sprang overboard from the superstructure.

Lamb bit his lip. They were only a matter of a couple of hundred yards from the tanker now – he could feel its flames begin to heat his wind-chilled face. Silhouetted thus against the roaring backcloth of the furnace on the stricken ship, *Rose* would make a perfect target for any lurking sub.

'Captain–' Doan began, his face contorted and pleading, 'aren't we going to–'

'Yes, we are,' Lamb interrupted brutally. 'Stop engines!'

'*Stop engines!*' Pollacks swung round, his face ashen and aghast. 'But sir, we'll be sitting ducks out here against those flames!'

'You heard me – stop engines,' Lamb

50

repeated, surprising himself with his own calmness. 'Then get over to port and keep a lookout for the sub, if there is one. You, Doan, get down there and supervise the operation. Use your loud-hailer and tell them to swim, float or row over to us. I'm not going to lower any boats.'

Doan breathed a sigh of relief. 'Ay, ay, sir.'

Pollacks did not move. Lamb pretended to busy himself with his binoculars, making a play of focusing them on the sinking tanker. Still Pollacks did not go. In the end Lamb lost patience. Grabbing the ashen-faced First Lieutenant by the shoulder and pushing him brutally into the corner so that the man at the helm could not hear what he was going to say, he hissed: 'Listen, Pollacks, you get down on that deck at once, or by God, I'm going to have you on a court-martial for insubordination.'

'But–'

'There are no bloody buts!' Lamb cried, his teeth gritted together with anger. 'We're going to save those poor sods over there, sub or no sub. Now get on with it!'

Now under the American's bellowed instructions, the younger men on the tanker were springing into the red-hued water on all sides and striking out for the stationary destroyer, while the older ones and the non-swimmers were frantically wrenching the carley floats loose and flinging them into the

51

sea before following them.

Lamb cupped his hands, and leaning over the bridge, shouted to Doan: 'Tell 'em to get a move on, will you Mr Doan! She's not going to last much longer. Speed it up!'

The first of the survivors were now being helped over the side, dragged up the rope nets by a score of willing hands or hooked up at the end of Degenhardt's boat-hook like so many fish, to collapse on the deck in exhaustion, while evil-smelling pools of diesel-tinged blood and seawater formed around their bodies.

Lamb gripped the bridge rail, his body tense, his nerves jingling, as he watched the first of the burning oil drip over the side of the rapidly sinking tanker and follow the slower swimmers and the men on the floats. It advanced with frightening rapidity, and then it enveloped the last float. The flames parted for an instant. In it the trapped men threw up their arms, rising to their feet, as if they were praying, before the flames joined again. Lamb caught a horrifying glimpse of the men leaping in a frenzied dance of death, their burning bodies galvanised into agonised action by the searing heat.

Lamb knew he must act – and act soon. But there were still a good fifty men struggling frantically in the water, striking out desperately for the rescue ship, screaming, their white blobs of faces turned up to the *Rose,* as if they were seeing paradise itself. Could he abandon them?

The tanker solved the problem for him, as she exploded in an ear-splitting roar. The *Rose* heeled crazily, her mast nearly touching the churning water, and when she righted herself again, the tanker had vanished and the fire had gone out. Nothing remained of the tragedy save the obscene belches of the air escaping from the sunken ship, exploding on the surface of the water, and the couple of score of seamen floating on it like so many dead goldfish in a bowl of blood.

Hesitating no longer, Lamb shook himself out of his shocked reverie and jumped to the telegraphs. Swiftly he signalled 'full speed ahead' and in doing so saved HMS *Rose.* The mine which the departing U-boat had planted in the destroyer's path bumped into her too late. Once, twice, three times it slammed into the destroyer's hull, the noise clearly audible to the suddenly tense stokers in the engine room.

Then just as the mine had passed between the screws and seemed destined for the open sea behind them, it exploded, bringing the *Rose* to a sudden halt.

Three hours later she limped into the river at five knots with a badly twisted propeller shaft, leaking fuel and her precious store of issue rum, to the ironic cheers of the dockyard workers, who had spent the last two months refitting her.

Lamb had handed the *Rose* over to the First Officer and Doan in order to prepare his report on the torpedoed tanker and his own craft. But he could not concentrate and in the end he dropped his fountain pen in disgust, his mood as black as the bodies of the tanker's survivors now being cleaned of the clinging diesel oil below. 'Blast and damn!' he hammered on the table so that his instruments rattled violently, 'what in the name of heaven is wrong with the bloody *Rose?*'

He received a partial answer to that question the following morning when the same bowler-hatted Geordie foreman who had signed over the destroyer to him a mere five days before said with ill-concealed satisfaction, 'Well, Captain, she gone and done it again, hasn't she?'

'I know that,' Lamb replied, 'but what's the damage – and how long is it going to take to repair it?'

'Fourteen days at least, Skipper – that is if the Unions will buy their lads doing so much overtime.'

Mentally Lamb told the Unions what they could do with their lads. But he contented himself with saying to the foreman, 'Can't

54

you do better than that?'

The foreman shook his head with pious solemnity. 'I'm afraid that's quite out of the question!'

'*Balls!*' was Lieutenant Commander John Lamb's sole reply as he strode away, fists clenched angrily and dug deep into his jacket pockets.

Thus that night Tyneside was full of HMS *Rose*'s crew celebrating the surprise gift of a gash★ shore leave. At the old Commercial the green hands boasted loudly over their shandies of their first taste of action to an admiring crowd of Geordies. In the Power House, the spivs, decked out in all their number one finery, sailed into the crowd of giggling factory girls like a bunch of latterday pirates, all hair oil and rakish sidechats, their caps perched carefully at the back of their gleaming quiffs.

But in the Black Swan, known to the Navy as the 'mucky duck', the older hands had to retire in the face of a group of sailors from one of the cruisers anchored in the river, who burst into the old song as soon as they had entered, with, 'They're poor little lambs, who have gone astray – *baa, baa, baa*'.

Outside in the thick darkness of the

★Meaning rubbish or free.

blackout, followed by the words of that taunting song, 'gentlemen matelots ... doomed from here to eternity ... *baa, baa, baa,*' Scouse looked gloomily at the searchlights poking their cold silver fingers into the night sky and turned sourly to Bunts. 'Cheeky buggers! Poor little lambs, indeed! That skipper of ours is trying his bloody best. How can he help it that he's got a ruddy shower for a crew, answer me that, Bunts?'

'Happen yer right, Scouse,' his mate commented, adding sagely, 'But yer must admit that that ship's got a ruddy jinx on it. If yer want my opinion, yon bugger'll never join the Fleet till this little lot's long over.'

TWO: *CALL TO ARMS*

'That's right, and what would a large contingent of ski troops be doing in the flattest part of Germany? I doubt if they need the boards for their unsavoury behaviour in the – er – knocking shops of Hamburg's red light district.'
Lieutenant Commander Ian Fleming to Admiral Godfrey, Head of Naval Intelligence, March 30th 1940.

ONE

On the afternoon that HMS *Rose* limped up the river Tyne, immaculate General Nikolaus von Falkenhorst strode purposefully up the steps of the new Berlin Reich Chancellery. At the head of the steps, the twin, black-clad, helmeted giants of the *Leibstandarte* smacked their steel-tipped boots down on the marble as one and came to the present. Von Falkenhorst touched his well-manicured hand to the glistening peak of his cap and passed into the echoing gloom of the Führer's own HQ.

The rest were already waiting in the anteroom: Admiral Raeder, wearing the high stiff collar of the old Imperial Navy; hard-faced Captain Krancke of the naval staff; and Major Oster from Canaris's Intelligence Service, monocle screwed in his eye, smoking a hand-made cigarette through an ivory cigarette holder, his long face set in the cynical, all-knowing look, which had so often irritated the head of the XXI Corps.

He acknowledged the two junior officers' salutes with a curt 'good afternoon' and turned immediately to Admiral Raeder, commander of the German Navy. 'Well,

Raeder, it looks as if it's on, doesn't it?'

The Admiral nodded and cleared his throat. 'Seemingly, General. And not before time. Wegener* was right, of course. If we had occupied Norway in 1914, we would have had a better base for the U-boats and, in fact, for the whole fleet. Wegener states quite clearly that it is the duty of the German Navy to protect the merchant fleet against enemy attack. Again the Tommies are trying to bottle us up in the Baltic and cut us off from the North Atlantic, the Norwegian coast – and above all the Swedish ore coming through Narvik–'

'Is it that important?' Falkenhorst interrupted, attempting to bring the Admiral's flow of words to an end. He knew just how absurdly taken up the Navy people were with Wegener's *Sea Strategy in the World War.* But at this particular moment he didn't want a damn lecture on the subject.

'Of course, it's *all*-important,' Raeder answered, his fat face flushing abit. 'If Narvik were to fall into enemy hands, that would mean the end of our Swedish ore and without that the German war industry would grind to a halt within a few weeks. In essence, Norway remains neutral. If she doesn't, or is threatened by the enemy, we must seize her in our own grip of steel.' He clasped his

*Admiral Wolfgang Wegener.

pudgy hands together, as if he were wrapping them around an enemy throat, while behind him, Oster blew a slow, contemptuous blue ring of smoke into the air.

Five minutes later the gigantic SS aide, who towered at least a head taller than even Falkenhorst, ushered them into the Führer's presence.

Adolf Hitler, the head of the German state, was flanked by his two military advisers, cold-faced Colonel-General Jodl and heavy-jawed Field Marshal Keitel. But, as usual, it was the ex-infantry corporal and not the professional military men who gave the orders.

'General von Falkenhorst. In 1918 you led a landing operation in Finland. You are familiar with the area and the type of operation. What is the key element, in your opinion, that goes to make up the success of such an operation?'

Falkenhorst did not hesitate. Had he not spent the last twenty-odd years explaining the Finland Landing and similar operations to any junior officer prepared to listen in the mess? 'The essential thing, *Mein Führer* is the element of surprise. Even small, well-disciplined and well-equipped forces can achieve decisive results against a panic-stricken population – and military form-ations which lack the backbone and discipline that can only be gained in com-bat. Fear, uncertainty and the confusion

61

EXERCISE WESER (THE PLAN)

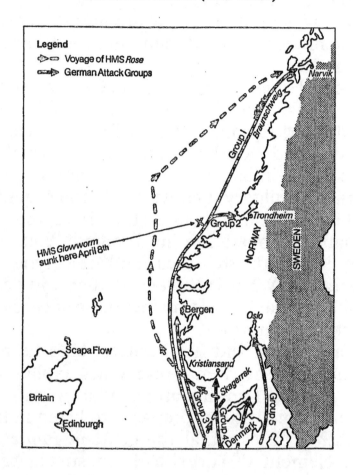

Legend
⇨ Voyage of HMS *Rose*
▭▶ German Attack Groups

Narvik

Braunschweig

Group 1

Group 2

Trondheim

NORWAY

SWEDEN

HMS *Glowworm*
sunk here April 8th

Bergen

Oslo

Scapa Flow

Kristiansand

Skagerrak

Britain

Group 3

Group 4

Group 5

Edinburgh

Denmark

which comes with them will be our allies!'

Adolf Hitler stroked his jaw thoughtfully for a moment, while the high-ranking officers stared at him in tense expectation. Outside the brutal, beer-and-schnapps-thickened voice of the guard commander ordered the new sentries of the *Leibstandarte* to their positions at the head of the steps.

Finally he spoke. *'Mein Herren,* your papers have convinced me. We shall attack Denmark and Norway in exactly four weeks' time. You, Falkenhorst, will be in charge of the operation.' He paused momentarily and looked up at the tall General as if he expected some objection. None came. 'Good. I shall expect you to report to me again in two weeks' time with the detailed operation planning. Naturally you will have the assistance of the *Kreigsmarine* and Intelligence.' He picked up the thick red pencil with which he marked his maps, and pointed it challengingly at the other officers.

Raeder and Oster nodded.

'Schoen.'

'And the code-name of the Operation, *mein Führer?'* Major Oster ventured. 'For security reasons, you understand?'

Adolf Hitler smiled. 'I have decided the operation will be called Exercise Weser*That

---

Weseruebung in the original German, the reference being to the North German River Weser.

63

should fool the Tommies.' With a gesture of finality, he dropped the round pencil on the map of the North lying in front of him on the great desk. It rolled a little way until it came to a rest, its blood-red point facing Narvik. The interview was over.

'Exercise Weser', Admiral Canaris, Head of German Intelligence, echoed the words slowly, stroking the beloved dachshunds which were as he had assured his fellow conspirator Oster often enough in these last eighteen months of intrigue and counter-intrigue the only living things he trusted in this world. 'So it has started, eh, Oster?'

Major Oster took the black ivory cigarette-holder out of his mouth. 'What can you expect from the Bohemian corporal, sir? Neutrality is just a word for him – he has no scruples. *Heaven, arse and twine!*' he cursed, using the soldiers' oath, his rage breaking through the veneer of cynicism. 'Why the devil didn't we kill him in '39 when we had the chance!'

Canaris, the 'Old Fox', as his agents called him behind his back, the ex-submarine commander who had reputedly once made love to the great Mata Hari herself, allowed himself a quiet smile. 'Because, my dear Major Oster, we didn't have the courage of our convictions. Or if you want it more crudely – we simply didn't have the guts!'

64

He rose to his feet a little awkwardly, cradling a fat dachshund under each arm, and walked to the window of his second-floor office in the Intelligence Division's *Tirpitzufer* HQ. For a moment he stared out at the fat slugs of barrage balloons guarding the German capital's administrative and diplomatic quarter. 'I see they've got a flak battery on the roof of the building next to the Danish Embassy,' he said carefully. 'Eighty-eights, I think. Make an awful racket when they open up. I wonder what our friends the Danes think about it?'

Oster stared at his chief's back, wondering what the Old Fox, who like himself was dedicated to overthrowing the Hitler regime, was getting at.

'But there again, in a month or so's time, there will be no Danish Embassy in Berlin and that particular little problem will be solved.' He turned round suddenly, his cunning dark eyes searching Oster's face, a faint grin on his face. 'I wonder what our friend the Danish military attaché would say to that, if he knew, eh, Oster?'

'I don't know, Admiral,' Oster stuttered, still puzzled.

'Of course, the whole business might not come off,' the Admiral continued, while Oster stared up at him, 'if the people in the North knew what was coming. I mean, let us just suppose that the Norwegians, for example, suddenly mobilised in advance, immobilised most of their airfields, mined their territorial waters. What do you think Jodl's reaction would be, if Intelligence could pass concrete details to him?'

'He'd advise Hitler to call the operation off!'

'And a lot of German lives would be saved. It might also give us another chance to get a reliable team together to arrange for the Bohemian Corporal's sudden departure from this world. I feel–'

'But how, Admiral?' Oster interrupted.

Carefully Admiral Canaris stroked the dachshund under his left arm. 'Well, I thought you went riding with Kjoelsen* every morning in the *Tiergarten* park. He's a very good man, reliable, keeps his mouth shut.' Suddenly he stopped stroking a dachshund, iron in his voice. 'He's your man. Tell him about Exercise Weser.'

Thus is was that a group of young naval officers assembled in Room 39 of the Admiralty Building in Whitehall to make a decision which would go to the First Lord himself.

'You see,' Admiral Godfrey, the tall, heavy-set Head of Naval Intelligence, lectured his

*The Danish Military Attaché Rear-Admiral Kjoelsen.

smart-faced young men, 'I don't want to stick my neck out and alert the First Sea Lord if this thing is only a plant. You know what he is, when he's angry? He'd have my guts for the proverbial garters!'

There was a rumble of laughter from the assembled Intelligence officers; they all knew to their cost about the 'old man's' explosive temper.

'But why should we disbelieve this Danish chap Kjoelsen,' objected one of them. 'What advantage would he gain by leading us up the garden path, sir?'

'Well, the Danes don't particularly like us at the moment since we mined Danish waters last month. I don't see why they should help us particularly.' He turned to the elegant Lieutenant Commander lounging at the tall French window, which overlooked the private entrance to No 10 Downing Street, moodily puffing one of his handmade three-ringed Morland Specials. 'What's your opinion, Ian?'

Commander Ian Fleming turned slowly, his long, sardonic face heavy with thought. For a moment he did not speak, as though he were still making up his mind about what he was to say. Finally he said, 'I think it's the real thing, sir. The Boche are going to attack – and the thing that clinches it for me is that we have a report from one of our agents in Hamburg – he keeps what is commonly known as a knocking shop in the *Reeper-bahn.*' He paused to let them laugh, 'That most of his army customers over the last seven days have been *Gebirgsjaeger.*'

'*Gebirgsjaeger?*' Godfrey echoed. 'What are they when they are at home, pray?'

'Bavarians and Austrians, sir, chaps who run around in leather shorts and indulge in yodelling in peace-time – and don skis in wartime when the Army needs them.'

'*Skis!*'

'That's right,' Fleming pressed home his advantage, 'and what would a large contingent of ski troops be doing in the flattest part of Germany? I doubt if they need the boards for their unsavoury behaviour in the – er – knocking shops of Hamburg's red light district.'

Godfrey's eyes lit up. 'Of course – *Norway,* you mean, Ian?'

'Right in one, sir. Why else?'

Admiral Godfrey hesitated no longer. 'All right, Ian, you've sold me the idea. Get the First Lord on the blower and put me on the scrambler.'

His Lordship acted with that swift flamboyance that was going to make him famous in the difficult years to come. As soon as he placed down the phone, he picked up a single sheet of Admiralty notepaper and began scribbling rapidly on it in his

68

characteristic, flowing hand: *'Alert all light craft not on convoy duty. Speed up commissioning trials of all destroyers. Bring every refit to an end immediately. Every available destroyer is to report to an active service squadron forthwith. Pray, give me the ships I require NOW!'*

The portly little man with the red face of one who has imbibed too much vintage port, hesitated an instant, then with a flourish he set his name under the message, *'Winston S. Churchill.'*

Thus it was that at the end of a strange chain of events, the old destroyer HMS *Rose* sailed into Plymouth on the last day of March 1940, to join the Eighth Destroyer Flotilla to the accompaniment of a slow handclap from the matelots lining the decks of the other destroyers and a derisive chorus of 'baa, baa, baas'.

*'Rose'*s baa-lambs', as the crew of the jinx ship were already being called throughout the Fleet, had come to go to war.

TWO

Captain (D) F. Vernon Yorke, DSO, the Commander of the Eighth Destroyer Flotilla, did not look up when Lamb marched into his office in the Royal Navy Barracks at Devonport overlooking the bright harbour lined with cranes and the dark grey hulls of his destroyers. Instead he continued writing on the paper set in front of him on the big desk, arranged with such methodical precision that an observer might have concluded that Captain Yorke spent a good deal of his time prior to getting down to work in the morning measuring out exactly where each individual item on it should be placed.

For what seemed a long time the grey-haired, hook-nosed officer with his left eye socket covered by a black patch, continued writing, while Lamb licked his lips, a little embarrassed, and wondered whether this descendant of admirals of the fleet who had fought Britain's battles since the days of Nelson always treated his new skippers with such obvious discourtesy.

Finally, however, the Commander of the Eighth Flotilla put down his wooden,

Government-issue pen and looked at the young officer coldly. For the first time Lamb got a full view of his martinet's face, from the singular, icy-blue eye to the haughty mouth heavy with High Church piety and bitterness at still being a captain of destroyers instead of an admiral after thirty years' service.

'Lamb, isn't it,' he asked unnecessarily, his voice as sombre and as unfriendly as his face. 'Lamb of HMS *Rose?*'

'Yessir.'

'Hm,' the Flotilla Commander said slowly, his lips pursed. 'I might as well tell you, Commander, that I did not request that the *Rose* should be attached to my flotilla. Indeed, when their Lordships informed me of their decision, I protested most strongly. You understand that?'

Lamb flushed. He knew that in the Royal Navy, captains were supposed to be only a few grades below God Almighty; but he thought this was going a little too far. 'No, I don't understand, sir,' he answered firmly. 'Why *did* you object, if I may be so bold as to ask?'

Captain Yorke's icy expression did not change. The only sign of any inner tension was the drumming of the fingers of his left hand on the desk. 'Because your ship is too slow. It will not be able to keep up with my Tribals... And your crew, according to the

71

information in my possession, is little better than an untrained rabble.

'In addition, I am not impressed by your own performance as a captain since you took over the *Rose*.' He held up a heavy hand, as if he wished to stifle any protestation Lamb might make. 'However, I'm stuck with you and the *Rose* and I shall have to make the best I can of it. Tomorrow, you will begin a new series of immediate exercises – under my personal supervision. That is all. Good day, Commander.' With that he bent his head over his papers, leaving Lamb standing there, red-faced, angry and completely bewildered.

If the crew of the *Rose* had thought that Lieutenant Commander Lamb was a hard taskmaster during the three days of the working-up trials, they now discovered that Captain (D) Vernon Yorke was a veritable Bligh, who worked them from dawn to dusk without mercy. In the next few days, as the winter began to give way to a balmy spring, life aboard the *Rose* became one long, hectic round of speed trials, special stand-tos, shoots and trials of seamanship under Captain Yorke's malicious supervision. On the first morning he came aboard as six bells summoned the first watch to its duties. Dragging an unhappy Pollacks, who was lingering over a coffee in the wardroom, with him, he insisted on inspecting the lower decks, heavy with the smell of unwashed bodies and stale food. That morning he took fifteen men's names for having left their hammocks slung and ordered Pollacks to give each of them five days' slack hammock drill.

That day they ran into bad weather, with the sea water pouring down the ammunition hoists by the ton and flooding the lower mess decks, already littered with personal possessions and smashed china mugs brought down by each fresh roll of HMS *Rose*. Apparently tireless, however, Yorke insisted on making another snap inspection with Pollacks as they sailed wearily back into Plymouth to find the decks covered with off-watch sailors who had flopped down on the wet, debris-littered floors and fallen into an exhausted sleep.

'Get that rabble up, Mr Pollacks!' he barked, his hook-nose crinkled in disgust. 'Get them up at once! I will not have the men of my flotilla resting, even if they are off duty, before the messdecks are thoroughly dried, cleaned and thoroughly ventilated, with all wet clothing hung up to dry. My men will not behave like pigs!' And with that he was striding imperiously away leaving Pollacks to the unenviable task of rousing the sleep-drunken, grumbling sailors.

On the second day, Captain Yorke supervised the bridge while Doan and Lamb took the *Rose* out of Plymouth harbour. There was a bitter northerly wind sweeping in from Drake's Island; outside the harbour the sea boiled angrily and leaped at the weathered blocks of the sea wall. Yet Lamb was quite satisfied that the young HO rating at the wheel could handle the job of taking the ship out by himself.

Yorke wasn't. 'There's a strong tide running this morning, Lamb,' he snapped, lowering the binoculars with which he had been surveying the deck below, 'and the light is not good. Are you going to entrust the job to him?' He indicated the tense young rating with a curt nod.

'Yessir,' Lamb said firmly, his face set and angry. 'He knows his job.'

'I see. Well, it's on your head. But I must point out to you that one of your quarter-deck party is out of the rig of the day, Lamb. Take his name!'

Lamb bit back the angry retort just in time. How could Yorke bother with such trivialities at a moment like this? Still he swung round on Doan, who was staring at Yorke's back incredulously. 'Take that man's name, please, Mr Doan.'

Nervous as he was, the young rating at the wheel safely negotiated the tricky exit to the harbour, against the fast running tide, slapping the vicious black rocks which were only a matter of yards away from their port bow. But Yorke had not finished.

As Doan reported to him: 'Fo'c'sle secured for sea, sir,' he snapped: 'All right, Mr Doan, let's have every man at action stations. I want to ascertain if every one of them knows his station. *At once!*'

'But, sir, that has already been done,' Lamb intervened, his voice full of barely repressed anger and defiance.

Yorke did not even look at him. Instead he stared fixedly at Doan and barked: 'Well then we'll do it again, won't we?'

'Do you know, skipper?' Doan said that night after Yorke had gone ashore to his quarters and the officers sat hunched morosely over large pink gins in the ward-room, 'that guy seems to have it in for you personally.'

'You shouldn't say that, Doan,' Lamb replied wearily, trying to feign a loyalty he did not feel. 'After all, he is our Flotilla Commander.'

'But it's true, skipper. I watched him this morning on the bridge as he went out and he was watching you with that bloody hawkeye of his, as if he were praying that you would make a balls-up of it. Honest!'

'Oh, don't talk such rot!' Lamb retorted.

But later that night, as he took off his shoes and jacket wearily and tumbled into his bunk, hoping to grab a few hours' sleep before another day with Yorke commenced, he knew the American was right. Captain (D) Vernon Yorke, DSO, really did want him and the *Rose* to fail.

On the morning after the last day of the exercises, Yorke himself appeared to attend the compulsory Sunday service held on the lower deck. He was armed with a prayer of his own composition, and completely un-abashed by the fact that a quarter of the sullen, obstinately un-Christian, bareheaded men facing him were on some kind of charge or other on his account, he proceeded to read it to the crew in his emotionless voice, 'Oh God, our loving Father and Comfort, bless us in our efforts to make this an efficient ship in your service...'

'Christ, just listen to his nibs,' Scouse whispered angrily to his oppo Bunts. 'Ruddy hypocrite! What the hell does he think God is – a bloody Admiral of the Fleet!'

Supremely unaware of the lower deck's reaction, Yorke continued, invoking them to, 'keep in mind the real causes of this terrible new war – dishonesty, greed, selfishness and the lack of love'.

'Ay, he can say that again,' Scouse quipped, 'it's been so long since I had a bit of how's-yer-father, I've forgotten what it's like!'

Coxswain Degenhardt withered him with a look.

'Let us therefore,' intoned the Flotilla Commander piously, 'drive them out of this ship so that she may be a pattern of the new life after this war for which we are fighting. Make His Majesty's Ship *Rose*, O God, thy righteous weapon with which to smite down thy enemies. Amen.' He bowed his head, as if overcome by emotion.

It was fortunate that he did so. For there was nothing pious about the looks on the faces of the men he had persecuted during the last few days, as they mumbled under their breath. 'A-*bloody*-men!'

When Yorke raised his head again, his face was set in its usual cold expression. 'Before I leave the ship, I want to say a few words to you,' he barked, sweeping his single eye along their bare-headed ranks, the wind from the Sound whipping the collars of their jackets against the backs of their neck and rippling the bellbottoms in wild shivers. 'This afternoon I have been ordered to attend the Admiralty and I can guess what I shall be told there.' He paused deliberately, while the crew, suddenly attentive, hung on his words. 'The Eighth Flotilla will be ordered into action – I don't know where. And even if I did, I wouldn't be able to tell you, naturally. But action it will be!'

Doan flashed Lamb a swift look. But

77

Lamb had no eyes for the American. His gazed was fixed on his Number One's face, set in a look of abject dread.

'Now, as you have probably guessed,' Captain Yorke was saying, 'I was not pleased with the performance of this ship when she was first attached to my flotilla and even after the last few days, I'm little better satisfied.'

Lamb flushed angrily, knowing that Captain Yorke was deliberately humiliating him in front of the crew.

'Unfortunately, time has run out and I shall have to take HMS *Rose* as she is. But let me say one more thing,' he raised his right forefinger, as if in warning. 'The lives of my trained crews depend upon you men, valuable lives which will be needed in the battle to come. As a result I will tolerate no failure, no weakness, no incompetence which might endanger those lives. I want it to be perfectly understood that I shall punish most stringently the slightest mistake of anyone on board the *Rose* – and I mean anyone.' For a long moment, his gaze swept over and rested on Lamb's angry face; then he tore it away as if by an effort of will and cried: 'Now we shall sing Hymn Number Five in the book – *Oh God, our help in ages past...*'

THREE

On the morning of Tuesday, April 2nd, the officers of the Eighth Destroyer Flotilla filed past the Petty Officer guarding the companionway, checking their identity cards, and began to assemble in the glittering new wardroom of Captain Yorke's own ship HMS *Defiance*. Excitedly the junior officers chattered among themselves, regaling each other with the latest 'buzzes',* ranging from action in the Med against the Italians who were soon expected to join the war on Hitler's side, to routine convoy duty in the North Atlantic. For their part, the captains confined themselves to brisk professional remarks about the state of the war. But Lamb, feeling somewhat of a new boy among them, could see that they, too, were infected by heady excitement at the prospect of impending action.

Captain Yorke entered at precisely nine o'clock with a bundle of charts under his arm, laid his cap down exactly in the corner of the cleared table and flashed a cold look around their ranks, as if he were making

*Rumours.

sure there was no interloper among them. 'Let me emphasise that I expect you, all of you, including the junior officers, to bear in mind that what I have to say now is absolutely top secret.' He nodded to the poster on the wardroom wall which advised that 'Careless Talk Costs Lives'. 'Please bear that in mind.'

There was a murmur of assent and some of the assembled officers fiddled with their cigarette cases and pipes, making it obvious that they wished the Destroyer Flotilla Commander to give them permission to smoke before he settled down to the briefing.

But instead Captain Yorke nodded to his first officer, who took one of the charts Yorke had brought with him and attached it to the bulkhead. 'The Baltic, Denmark and Norway. Our future area of operations!'

Yorke silenced the excited buzz of talk among the officers with one swiftly raised eyebrow. 'Now, then, this is what the First Lord ordered to be done on Sunday. The Second Destroyer Flotilla under War-burton-Lee is to cover a planned minelaying operation in the Norwegian Leads. Escorted by his ships, the minelayers will, when the order is given, mine the Westfjord approach to the Norwegian port of Narvik. Other minelayers will carry out the same operation between Trondheim and Bergen. Now why, you will naturally ask, why are we planning to carry out this mining of neutral waters? Because Intelligence has good reason to believe that the Boche are about to invade that country and it is vital that we prevent them gaining control of the iron-ore port of Narvik!' He sat back momentarily in his red-leather padded chair. Doan flashed a triumphant look at Lamb. 'Did you hear that, skipper? We're gonna mix it at last!' he whispered urgently.

Lamb grinned back at the former 'lootenant, junior grade', pleased at his undisguised enthusiasm.

'Now the forces in the far north of Norway will only be standing by for the time being until the moment the Boche actually move. Technically the Norwegians are still neutral and we must, of course, observe that neutrality till the very last minute. Besides, once the Boche do act, we'll easily beat them to the north. It is different in the case of Denmark. Once the Boche invasion fleet moves out of its ports in North Germany – at Bremen, Hamburg, Emden – here, here and here – we'll have little chance of stopping their transports, etc., by mines. Thus, however distasteful it may seem to you, we must start mining Danish waters before the Boche moves. The First Lord had ordered, therefore, that the Eighth Flotilla should begin that particular operation before the invasion commences by mining Danish territorial waters between Norway and Denmark in the Skagerrak – here – in order to prevent the three infantry divisions, which the Boche intend to move by sea, from getting to Oslo.'

Yorke looked around their tense faces, as if he half expected some form of protest at this breach of neutrality and, although he heartily disliked the man, Lamb could see that Yorke's piety was not a pretence. He obviously had a genuine deep moral sense.

But no protest was forthcoming from these men, most of whom had spent their whole lives preparing for this moment. Yorke continued. 'This then is my plan. The four Ds, including my own flotilla leader, will be converted to mine-sweeping over the next twenty-four hours.' Lamb knew he referred to the flotilla's four Tribals of the 'D' class – *Defiance, Daring, Destruction* and *Darling,* all of which could be converted swiftly to carry sixty mines. 'We shall go in at night and plant a genuine minefield here – and a false one – here – just in case we need a mine-free passage through the Skagerrak later. Naturally the operation will have to be carried out with the utmost speed and dispatch during the hours of darkness. Let me stress that. *We must get in and out before dawn.* With the load of mines we shall be carrying we shall be slowed down considerably if we run into trouble. That, in essence, gentlemen, is the bare bones of our mission. Now, questions, please?'

Collins, a big raw-boned, pleasant-faced Lieutenant-Commander who commanded the *Daring*, was first off the mark. 'What kind of opposition can we expect, sir – and from whom?'

'A good question, Collins. A week or so ago, I think we could have expected some trouble from the Danes – after all, we shall be mining their territorial waters. But as the First Sea Lord said to us on Sunday – "the neutrals console themselves with the belief that the Allies will win the war and respect international law, and that the Germans are the only people who violate it... They all hope that the storm will have blown itself out before it is their turn to be gobbled up." Now apparently the Danes know from one of their own people in Berlin that the Boche intend to invade them sooner or later. As a result, Intelligence thinks we won't have much trouble from them.'

Collins smiled faintly. 'It wasn't exactly the Danes I was worrying about, sir. I was thinking of the Jerries.'

'Well, you may be sure *they* won't respect Danish territorial waters, once the balloon goes up. But I doubt if they'll have any heavy stuff up in the Skagerrak once we move in.

'Now, any more questions before I give you your orders and let you go on your way to do your planning? No? Then I think we should dismiss–'

'Sir.' It was Lamb, his face set and determined, who had dared interrupt Captain Yorke. All eyes flashed to him. Somewhere a junior officer giggled like a shocked schoolgirl.

'Yes, Commander,' Yorke said coldly.

'May I ask what role the *Rose* will play in this operation, sir?'

'Ah, yes, the *Rose*,' Captain Yorke said the name as if he were aware of it for the very first time. Then he raised his voice while Collins looked at Lamb, his eyes full of sympathy. 'Well, as you know, the *Rose* is some five knots slower than the Ds. Therefore I can't expect you to go in with the rest of us. It would be too dangerous for you if we run into trouble. You understand?'

'Yessir,' he persisted stony-faced. 'But my role?'

'The role? Well, it was decided at the Admiralty – on my advice– that you would position yourself here,' he indicated the spot on the big chart, 'just off the coast of Denmark in the entrance to the Skagerrak, just in case the Boche decides to interfere, though as I have already stated, I think that eventuality is hardly likely.'

Lamb caught a fleeting glimpse of his

officers' faces. The two subs were frankly bewildered by what was going on in front of them. Pollacks's face bore a look of undisguised relief, but Doan's was sullen with disappointment.

'You mean, sir, that we shall not take part in the actual operation?'

Yorke nodded. 'You could put it like that, if you wished, Lamb. Now, then, gentlemen, I think it would be better if you went back to your ships. Jenkins here,' he indicated his first officer, 'will give you your envelopes with the more detailed orders. We sail at dusk tomorrow evening.'

The next twenty-four hours passed in frantic activity, as they prepared for a mission which would take them to sea for at least a couple of weeks. Ammunition barges came alongside and sweating deck crews were kept busy loading cases of five-inch shells. The NAAFI rations – duty-free cigarettes and tobacco – were loaded under the supervision of eagle-eyed customs officers, who watched the cases of 'coffin nails' and 'Navy cut', as if they expected a squad of black marketers to appear at any moment and begin selling them to the local dockies. They were followed by case after case of 'Old Mother Jamieson's Farmhouse Dinner', known on the lower deck as 'Old Mother Jamieson's Farmhouse Dog', or more simply as 'bow-wow' because of the quality of the meat in the big cans. A little later a mysterious cardboard container was rejected by Degenhardt when he discovered it held several gross of rubber contraceptives.

As he snapped angrily at the red-faced matelot from the Quartermaster's who had brought it on board, 'What do you think we're gonna do out there – fight or fornicate?'

In the middle of the morning, the 'Gestapo' arrived on board – four hard-faced Naval Policemen from the Barracks – dragging with them two shame-faced leading hands, minus their trousers.

'Found them sneaking out of the Snake Pit an hour ago, Coxswain,' one of the police explained. 'Said they was trying to get back to their ship – without their pants on!' He sniffed disdainfully. 'In the knocking shops down there more likely.' He thrust the release form at Degenhardt, 'Here you are, Coxswain, sign here.'

Degenhardt signed for 'the bodies' and let the police leave the ship before hissing at the trouserless ratings. 'You know what yer can get for this, don't you – desertion when we are just gonna go on active service – *death!*'

'But Coxswain,' Scouse pleaded, 'we was trying to get back to our ships on time – honest.' He gulped. 'Ask Bunts–'

'Don't tell me, tell the skipper,' Degenhardt cut him short. 'Off you go below and get your spare pants. I'm going to wheel you in front of the Captain in five minutes exactly.'

'Caps off!' Degenhardt bellowed five minutes later as he wheeled the two ratings into the Captain's cabin.

'Well?' Lamb demanded. 'Let's have it and have it quick.'

As usual it was Scouse who did the talking in his fast nasal Liverpool accent. They had gone ashore with one of the quartermaster launches to 'get a little bit of the other'. One thing had led to the other, but when they had attempted to leave, the 'judies didn't want to let us go, sir. They swore the *Rose* was a jinx ship – all them tarts down the Pit know more about the Fleet than the average three-striper. They said we should stay with them in the knocking-shop – er, their establishment. All we'd get, if the Gestapo nicked us would be seventy-four days in the glasshouse and that was better any old day than going down with the sodding *Rose*. That's what they said, didn't they, Bunts?'

'But we was having none of that, sir. I told them not to come the old acid with us – and then later, when we was gonna leave, they nicked our bell-bottoms. So what was we to do, I ask you? I knew we had to get back to the ship before she sailed – so off we went without pants, with half the Pit hanging out

87

of the windows laughing their stupid heads off'n us.'

Lamb caught himself just in time, or he might have been forced to do the same. Yet, at the same time, he was oddly touched. The Leading Hand was right. All they would have risked by absenting themselves from the *Rose* would have been a comparatively light sentence in the Chatham Naval Prison; yet, despite the *Rose*'s reputation, they had made it back in time.

'All right,' he snapped, 'I haven't got time to go into detailed explanations. Fourteen days on return to port. For the time being, off you go back to your own stations.'

Scouse and Bunts saluted him, as if he were the First Lord himself and were wheeled out again, grateful smiles on their faces.

Thus the hours flew by and it was only when the last mailboat was about to leave the *Rose*, that Lamb suddenly realised he had not written a final note to his mother. Hastily he grabbed a piece of notepaper and scribbled an explanation on it, ending with, 'we've had a hard time over the last week, but I am growing more confident in them. The pressures of the last few days have unified them somehow.' He thought of the two ratings running the gauntlet of the red light district without their pants in order to get back to their ship and knew instinctively

88

that he was right. He added the last few words almost with a flourish. 'When the balloon really goes up, I know the men won't let me down!'

As the early spring dusk started to close in, hiding the further reaches of the harbour, and transforming the hills of Plymouth's hinterland from purple to black, while the buoys began to light up as if by magic, the Eighth Flotilla nosed its way out of Plymouth.

From Drake's Island the strength of the salt breeze increased, ruffling the surface of that same Sound which had seen the Great Admiral go out to do battle with the Armada four centuries before. Carefully they picked their way through the anchorage crowded with light cruisers and escort vessels of all shapes and sizes, a brave sight reminding Lamb, poised on the bridge, of the power and might of the great Empire of which he was a member.

Slowly but surely the five destroyers began to pick up speed, Yorke's *Defiance* in the van. Now the four D-class destroyers were hitting each wave as if it was something solid, their forecastle awash with the white water which surged over their port bows. The *Rose* tore along in their wakes across a surface already whipped into a frothy cream by the four destroyers in front of her. But Lieutenant-Commander John Lamb did not mind being the last ship, playing the role of 'tail-end Charlie' to which Captain Yorke had assigned him so contemptuously. Indeed, at that moment, he was seized by a kind of heady excitement that would have caused him to shiver if he had not pulled himself up in time. He was going into battle in charge of his own ship.

Then the night descended upon the land behind them. England disappeared, and they were alone with the sea and the unknown dangers ahead.

THREE: *BAPTISM OF FIRE*

'It is for that reason and what happened this morning in the Strait, Commander Lamb, that I am recommending you for a court-martial as soon as we return to port. The charge will be cowardice in the face of the enemy.'

Captain Vernon Yorke
to Lieutenant-Commander Lamb.
April 6th 1940.

ONE

On the afternoon of their second day out from Plymouth, they arrived at the mouth of the Skagerrak, some six or seven miles off the coast of North Jutland, their presence concealed only by the thin grey fog that masked the coast.

It had been an uneventful trip. They had not sighted a single ship once they had cleared the Channel and entered the North Sea, and now both the pewter-coloured sky and the green sea were devoid of aircraft and ships.

As the rest of the Ds began to slacken speed, HMS *Defiance* swung round in a graceful white arc and headed towards the *Rose* at thirty knots.

'Just look at him,' Pollacks said sourly to Doan, as the *Defiance* swept towards them in a sweeping white wash of foam. 'It's almost as if the hard-nosed bugger wants to show us how damned slow we are!'

'Yeah, you can say that again. But–'

'Switch on the loud-hailer, Doan,' Lamb cut into their conversation, as the *Defiance* turned in a flurry of foam, and slowing down, began to edge towards them. 'Captain

Yorke's coming alongside.'

From the lower deck of the *Defiance*, out of sight of the bridge, there came the faint bleating chorus of 'baa baas'. On the gun-deck Scouse and his crew, suddenly red in the face, began to give their taunters the new V-sign.

'Get on to those men down there, Cox-swain,' Lamb bellowed. 'I want that stopped at once!'

'Ay ay, sir,' Degenhardt snapped and doubled away.

The *Defiance*'s loud-hailer crackled into electric life. 'Can you hear me over there, *Rose?*' Yorke's harsh voice demanded.

'Yes, Captain,' Lamb replied, pressing the button.

'Good. Well, this is the parting of the ways. We'll start our approach soon. Take station here and keep a weather eye open for the Boche, though I should imagine you'll have a quiet night of it. We'll rendezvous with you again at dawn on the morrow. Clear?'

'Clear, sir. And may I wish you the best of luck?'

There was a moment of hesitation, then Yorke called coldly, 'Thank you, Lamb.'

Somewhere in the *Defiance* an engine-room telegraph clanged, then the destroyer seemed to jump away. Minutes later she and the rest of the Ds had vanished into the coastal mist, leaving Lamb staring after them and wishing that he was going with them.

But he did not show his feelings to his fellow officers as he briefed them a few minutes later in the wardroom. 'So you see,' he concluded, just as the sun was beginning to slip over the horizon, a sickly-yellow ball that lay there for a moment, as if too exhausted even to make that final effort, 'if Jerry *does* venture out – and Captain Yorke things he won't – it's my guess he'll be coming up from the south-west, Emden or Wilhelmshaven. There are *Schnellboot**** flotillas in both places as well as destroyers, according to Intelligence. My plan, then, is to creep in as close as possible to the coast – I don't want one of those nasty Jerry S-boats playing around with my bottom–'

There was a polite titter from the Subs.

'So that we'll have any potential enemy to port. Naturally we'll carry out our usual 'darken ship' drill, but tonight I want you all to be extra careful. I don't want any nosy Dane bothering us, even though they might be our allies before long. All clear?'

'All clear, sir,' they repeated, rising to get on with the job of blacking out the ship.

'And one more thing,' he added, his face suddenly very serious. 'Let's not get all resentful about our role in this business and

*German motor torpedo boats.

treat it simply as a realistic training exercise. It isn't! We are on active service. We must act accordingly. We've got to be one hundred per cent on our toes. After all, we might see action yet. All right, on your way, gentlemen.'

Pollacks's sneer of contempt at the way the young subs' faces brightened up was barely concealed. 'One day,' Lamb promised himself, 'I'm going to kick your behind – hard!'

A few moments later the public address system was piping out the order to darken ship, and as Lamb and Coxswain started on their rounds, the crew sprang to to carry out the job. Every companionway was blocked off to the outside by canvas screens; the galley fires were damped down; from now onwards only sandwiches and hot drinks would be served. Lights were dimmed everywhere, save in the engine room. Even the green glowing dials of the instruments on the bridge were toned down by the little wheels on their sides so that not even the faintest light would reveal their presence to prowling enemy ships. Then HMS *Rose* headed for the coastal fog bank like a lean, silent grey ghost.

But Lamb and Degenhardt were not fated to get far with their inspection. They had just reached the galleys and Degenhardt had hardly silenced one green hand singing monotonously over his chores 'Roll on the

Rodney, Nelson and *Renown,* this one funnelled bastard *Rose* is getting me down', with one murderous glance, when the ER9 in charge of the engines burst in, his face brick-red, his big raw hands thick with grease up to the wrists.

'Captain, captain,' he cried urgently. 'Can I speak to you?'

Lamb swung round. It struck him that it was the first time he remembered seeing the ancient Scottish chief in his grubby white overalls and scuffed canvas shoes out of his beloved engine room. 'What is it, Chief? Where's the fire?'

The ER9 had no time for pleasantries. 'The *Rose* has gone and let us down again, sir,' he answered, a little breathlessly. 'I've got a bearing running hot – red hot – on the main shaft, sir.'

Lamb felt his heart sink. He didn't say anything, though, for he knew what was coming.

'Ay, the wee bugger's as hot as hell,' the ER9 growled, so angry that he forgot he was addressing the Captain. 'Perhaps a blocked oil pipe or something o' the kind.'

'And?'

The ER9 tugged at the end of his bulbous nose, pitted with innumerable blackheads caused by the diesel oil he worked with all the time. Suddenly he was embarrassed.

'Well, sir, I'm afraid we'll have to shut

down the engines.'

Lamb could not conceal his disappointment. 'No, Chief, not that!'

'Ay, I'm afraid it is, sir,' the other man answered doggedly, his gaze down on his scuffed shoes. 'Yer see, sir, if we don't and there's no oil coming through, yon shaft'll seize up as sure as cats has kittens. And then we'll be really caught by the short and curlies – no, sir, there's no other way we can do it,' he added with an air of finality.

Lamb bit his bottom lip for a moment. To use the Chief's own phrase, they were caught by the short and curlies as it was, stuck in Danish territorial waters, with the possibility – remote according to Captain Yorke, but still there all the same – that the enemy might turn up during the time they were immobilised. 'How long will it take to do the job, Chief?'

The ER9 scratched the back of his cropped head, dislodging the Woodbine stump lodged behind his big ear. 'Three hours – four hours, I can't rightly say.'

Lamb fought back the desire to moan. 'All right, get on with it, Chief – and be as quick as you can. Off you go. You Coxswain,' he swung round on Degenhardt, as the ER9 hurried away back to his engine-room, cursing as he went, 'I want you to go through the whole ship and warn every single man that I'll have anyone on Defaulters who makes the slightest possible noise. No unnecessary talking below decks and plimsolls instead of seaboots. Those on duty on deck, tiptoes only and I don't care if they look like a lot of fairy queens on Shaftesbury Avenue. Got it?'

'Got it, sir!' Degenhardt snapped, fully aware of the danger they were in now, immobilised in the face of any possible attack.

While the ER9 and his stokers laboured in the engine room, their wooden mallets muffled in rags as they tried to find the point of obstruction in the many hundred yards of piping that ran all across in the crowded engine room, the *Rose* floated motionlessly in the grey fog, the water slapping mournfully against her sides, her crew on tenterhooks.

Lamb had the watches changed every half hour so that the look-outs were on their toes all the time. Below, 'Asdic' and 'Radar' sweated over their green glowing instruments, while Sub-Lieutenant Ferris crept back and forth on the tips of his toes, his eyes bloodshot with strain and anxiety.

Although Doan offered to relieve him, Lamb would not be moved from the bridge, for he knew that even seconds would be precious in an emergency. He simply could not take any chances. Instead he hunched there on the wooden, canvas-backed high chair in moody contemplation, cursing the

99

Rose at regular intervals and fighting the infantile temptation to chew his right thumbnail.

Once, he started violently at a burst of hammering from the engine room. 'Good grief,' he cursed, feeling his heart beating like a trip-hammer, 'what in the world is that for? Coxswain, get down there immediately and tell that crazy Scot that he'll be waking up Hitler himself in Berlin if he goes on making that kind of racket!'

Five minutes later, Degenhardt returned to report that there would be no more hammering, at least for the time being. They had located the rough area of the blockage which was causing the bearing to run hot and were now going to try to clear it with wire.

Lamb gave a heartfelt sigh of relief. 'Thank God for that, Coxswain!' he said gratefully. 'And how long?'

'Perhaps another hour, sir, at the most.' Degenhardt hesitated. 'Do you mind if I stay up on the bridge, sir?'

'Of course not.' Lamb looked at the battered-faced PO curiously.

'And do you mind if I ask you a question, Coxswain?' he asked, a little later, trying to take his mind of what was going on below.

'Sir.'

'How did you come to join the Royal – I mean I hope you don't think that's a too personal question?'

'Not at all, sir. I killed a man – that's why I joined, sir.' Degenhardt answered, his voice emotionless.

'Killed a man!'

'Yessir. A storm trooper – in a Kneipe in Cuxhaven, a sort of a pub. You see I was an Obermaat in the old German Navy in thirty-two, nothing to do with politics, just a straightforward Navy man. But the storm troopers wouldn't leave us alone – they were always after us when we were in port. Any-way to cut a long story short, I was involved with one of them in a pub. One thing led to another, he pulled a knife on me, I hit him with a schnapps bottle,' Degenhardt hesi-tated an instant, 'and he had a thin skull. They said it was self-defence at the court-martial, but still they put me on the beach. Privately my skipper, one of the old school, told me I'd better get out of Germany–'

'You mean desert?'

'Yessir, and while the going was good. The Nazis were gunning for me, you see. So there I was, sixteen years in the Kriegsmarine, on the beach, and likely to have a knife slid between my ribs at any moment.' He shrugged eloquently. 'So what could I do? I stowed away in the next British merchant marine ship that ran into Hamburg – you see my mother was English, and I spoke the language. Five years later I was naturalised

101

and joined the Royal almost straight away.'

He stopped, as if he thought that the Captain had heard enough, but when Lamb did not speak, he continued: 'Of course, it wasn't easy at first being a – er – Jerry. A lot of the old hands didn't like having me in the mess. But,' he glanced down at his hamlike fist and grinned, 'in the end I convinced them that I wasn't too bad for a squarehead. You know the rest, sir.'

Lamb shared his grin briefly. 'But, Coxswain, as far as I can gather from your record you haven't been in action against your fellow countrymen yet. I mean,' he hesitated, wondering how he should phrase his question, 'what if you–'

'Have to fight against my own people, sir?' Degenhardt completed it for him.

'Yes.'

'Well, sir, all Germans are not Nazis, as they make them out to be in the war pictures, but they've thrown in their lot with Hitler all the same – and well, as we used to say in German, *mitgegangen, mitgefangen, mitgehangen.* That means roughly, sir – you went with him, you got caught with him.' The Coxswain drew a deep breath, 'and you'll hang with him!' I'm English now. England took me in, fed me, gave me a job.' He rubbed his heavy gnarled knuckles against his fighter's chin. 'If I have to, I'll fight the Jerries, sir…'

It was nearly dawn. The sky was already tinged with the sullen grey which heralded the slow approach of the new day in those northern waters, and the fog was beginning to drift away in slow, reluctant wisps. But still the sweating, anxious Scots ER9 had not quite cleared the blockage.

By now, worn out by their night-long vigil, most of the crew had spent all their nervous energy. They slumped against the dripping bulkheads or sprawled face-down on their hammocks. Occasionally one of them would rage briefly at 'them bloody engineers' who had 'buggered up the engine'. But for the most part, they waited helplessly like penned-up sheep at the slaughterhouse, sunk in private and bitter thought, knowing that every minute which passed brought them closer to the dawn and even greater danger.

By contrast, while the crew fell into a state of worn apathy, Lamb found that he could not relax, although he had been on the bridge for nearly twelve hours now. Time and time again, he searched the grey wavering fog-bank, possessed by an uncanny feeling, which kept the small hairs at the back of his head standing up, that there was something out there, waiting for him.

Just before five, he could not stand it any longer. He lifted the cover off the voice pipe and snapped: 'Bridge here – is that you, Ferris?'

103

'Ay, ay!' Ferris's young voice was worn and a little shaky. Lamb told himself the responsibility for the ship's safety was weighing heavily on the spotty-faced Sub.

'Anything?'

'Anything what, sir?'

Lamb's temper flared for an instant. 'On the radar – anything on the radar screen, man!'

'No, sir, nothing,' Ferris replied, shaken a little by the Captain's sudden outburst. 'The coast isn't helping, but we are doing our best–'

'Of course you are. Sorry, Ferris, but I'm expecting Captain Yorke to rendezvous with us soon,' Lamb lied. 'Keep me in the picture, won't you?'

'Ay, ay, sir.'

He put the tube down and picked it up again almost at once. 'Bridge here. Engine room?'

'Ay, ay, sir,' the Scottish voice came through, heavy with decades of whisky-drinking and fatigue.

'Well?'

'Almost ready, sir. A wad of waste stuck up the ruddy pipe. God only knows how it got in there–'

'Thank God, Chief,' Lamb breathed out with relief. 'How long now?'

'Gimme five more minutes, sir. I've just got to–' But the ER9 never finished.

Suddenly another voice cut into Lamb's consciousness. *'Engine noise, sir. Bearing east!'* It was the port deck look-out.

In one and the same movement, Lamb clamped the cover down on the voice pipe and sprang to the other side of the bridge, suddenly wide awake. He cocked his head to one side. For a moment he couldn't hear anything. He strained hard. Then he heard it: the faint yet definite throb-throb of powerful engines – many of them. And he knew instinctively, even before the first of the ships came into view, that those engines did not belong to Yorke's destroyers.

TWO

The throb of the engines, muffled a little by the coastal fog, grew louder as the officers tensed on the bridge, eyes straining, seeking to penetrate the grey cloud in front of them. Suddenly Doan spotted the faint blue light winking to port.

'Over there, skipper – *to port*,' he hissed urgently, his voice low to prevent whoever it was in the strange ship from hearing him.

Lamb swept his night glasses round. Hurriedly he focused on the light. It was moving forward very slowly, as if searching for something. *For them?* A second later he knew his wild guess had been correct, as the first lean, low white-painted hull cut into the round circle of his glasses and with a shock of alarm he recognised the stark black and blood-red flag. The swastika of Nazi Germany.

'S-boats!' he said, trying to keep his voice under control. 'One, two, three–' He began to count the powerfully armed, 92-ton German motor torpedo boats, but an ashen-faced Pollacks beat him to it.

'My God,' he gasped, 'there are ten of them!'

The German craft were grouped in two groups of five, their white-painted, rakish hulls clustered together, as if they had arrived at their rendezvous. Swiftly Lamb ran his glasses over them. They were the latest class. He remembered having read about them in *Jane's Fighting Ships* – capable of doing forty knots and armed with two 21-inch torpedoes and two 20-millimetre Oerlikon cannon: even one could have been a tough proposition for an old ship like *Rose*. But now there were ten of them out there.

He pulled off the voice pipe cap. 'Bridge,' he whispered. 'Are you ready?'

'Ay, ay, sir,' the ER9 replied joyfully, still unaware of what was happening up above. 'All ship-shape and Bristol-fashion.'

'Good. Then I want all you can give me as soon as I give you the order.'

'Ay, ay, sir.'

'But you're not going to be fool enough–' Pollacks began, his eyes sick with fear.

Lamb did not give him time to finish. 'Of course I am.' He looked hard at his First Officer and snapped harshly, 'Sound action stations immediately.'

In a flash the heavy tension of the night was broken by the shrilling of the alarm bells. Heavy seaboots clattered across the wet metal decks, as the crew pelted to their duty stations. Down at the gun turrets the gun-layers were flinging themselves behind their rubber-cup sights. Above them the pom-pom gunners were strapping themselves in behind their 'chicago pianos', while their mates tossed heavy cases of shells on the deck beside them.

Lamb flashed one last look round the tense bridge and saw his men's faces glowing green in the light from the instruments. They were all at their stations, staring at him expectantly. Lamb said a quick prayer that neither they nor the *Rose* would let him down this time. Then he rapped out his order.

'Port, twenty-five! Full ahead together!'

As the helmsman wrenched at his wheel, Doan sprang forward and pushed home the telegraph. The ER9 responded immediately. He gave *Rose* the full benefit of her 30,000 horses. The destroyer vibrated like a crazy thing as she surged out of the fog.

Lamb thrust his face over the wind-break. 'Gowan!' he yelled above the sudden roar of the engines.

'Ay, ay, sir!'

'Stand by for surface action. Local control!'

'Local control it is, sir!' Gowan the Guns roared back, fighting to keep his balance as the plates trembled violently beneath his feet. He swung round, the sudden wind whipping at his slim figure. *'Turret A,'* he yelled, *'enemy craft Red eight-o... Turret B –*

Red eight-o-two!'
Scouse was the first off the mark. He pressed the button and the tons of steel which made the turret swing round, steadied, and levelled with the still unsuspecting S-boat. In front of him the young gun-layer, eye pressed to the telescope, sweating in spite of the dawn cold, hunched tensely over his controls. To his right the two rammers waited, while a third man, shoulders bent with the effort, cradled the yellow-gleaming 100-pound shell in his brawny bare arms. Now he waited, rattling off under his breath the first 'Hail Mary' he had said in many a year.

A second later B-turret found its target. Gowan dared not wait any longer. The cluster of almost stationary S-boats was less than two thousand yards away. They would hear the *Rose* at any moment. He wet his suddenly dry lips, took a deep breath and roared: *'Open Fire!'*

The twin 5-inchers of A-turret roared in frightening unison. Scarlet flame stabbed from their narrow gleaming muzzles. Smoke shot backwards out of the turret. An instant later the nearest S-boat rocked crazily from side to side. Gouts of crazily boiling water shot into the grey air and obscured the enemy craft. But when the water dropped again, Scouse let out a huge roar. Although their shells had dropped short, the red-hot shards of flying metal had taken their toll, tearing a great gap in the S-boat's bow and grotesquely twisting one of her Oerlikons like molten glass. Thick black smoke was pouring from her engine room.

'We've hit the bitch!' he screamed. *'Hit her!'*

Then as B-turret opened up with a thunderous crash, sending a shock wave across the violently trembling *Rose,* A-turret's loading tray thudded against the guns' open, steaming breeches. The rammers thrust the gleaming shells home. The breech blocks clicked shut metallically. They were ready to fire again.

But the Germans reacted quicker than Lamb had anticipated. A star shell hissed into the cold grey sky, bathing the *Rose* in its frozen light. Almost blinded, Lamb flung his hand to his eyes.

'Zig-zag, helmsman,' he cried.

As the S-boats broke in wild confusion like a flock of sea-ducks caught unaware, 20-millimetre shells began hissing in their direction – a solid glowing wall of fiery red and white.

The helmsman, his face lathered in sweat, swung the *Rose* desperately from side to side. Below, the five-inchers fired again. But the sudden manoeuvre had thrown them off. Their shells missed both the damaged S-boat and the other target. In huge gouts of steaming water, they fell harmlessly in the sea, three hundred yards away from their targets. Then the Oerlikon shells submerged them.

Lamb pulled himself to his feet to the cries of the wounded below on the deck, eyes taking in the ragged holes that had appeared everywhere around him. 'Helmsman,' he roared, 'keep zig-zagging!'

The helmsman, a thin trickle of dark blood beginning its course down the side of his wounded face, yelled, 'Ay, ay, sir!' His voice seemed to come from a long way away. Lamb shook his head and swallowed hard. Ahead of them the S-boats werc weaving in all directions, seeming to skim across the surface of the water as they hit top-speed, twin streams of white spurting up from their bows.

'Gowan,' he yelled desperately, 'get on to them!'

'But you can't go after them,' Pollacks crunched across the metallic debris, his face contorted with fear. 'You saw what kind of fire power they've got.' He grabbed hold of Lamb's arm. 'Captain, you simply can't!'

'Get out of my way!' Lamb roared. Viciously he slammed the first officer against the bridge. He turned to Doan. 'If this officer gets in my hair again, Doan, you have my authority to arrest him.'

'Ay, ay, sir,' Doan snapped. 'With pleasure, sir!'

Weakly Pollacks leaned back against the canvas screen looking as if he were going to be violently sick.

Lamb ignored him. There were other things to be done. Below A-turret, as usual, first off the mark, had begun firing wildly again. But still the gunners were fighting back. Next to B, Degenhardt bent over a groaning young rating, his face ripped down the middle by one of the red-hot shell fragments.

But there was no time for casualties. While the S-boats were scattering at forty knots, the one hit by A-turret was desperately trying to make smoke to cover its crippled departure. Lamb felt a burning rage. The bastard was not going to get away like that.

He cupped his hands around his mouth and roared above the hideous racket of the S-boat motors, 'Coxswain, double over to the gunners. Tell 'em to concentrate on the one hit!'

Degenhardt lowered the dying boy's head to the deck, resting it as best he could in a thick sticky pool of the boy's own blood.

The two turrets swung round almost immediately. The twin five-inchers crashed in action once more. Their shells tore the air apart with a sound like the ripping of thick canvas. The stricken S-boat shuddered violently. A ready-use locker spurted into flame. Her ammunition began to explode.

Red and white tracer zig-zagged crazily into the sky, turning the faces of the panic-stricken crew blood-red. Now they started to abandon her, dragging their wounded with them, fighting and jostling each other on the bloodied deck as they scrambled for the buckled rail. In a shrieking black plume of smoke another salvo hit the sinking craft. Cherry-red flames flickered at the heart of the smoke. The boat began to keel over. What was left of her shattered super-structure touched the greedy waves, already reaching up for their tribute in human bodies.

But Lamb, standing there on the bridge transfixed with the horror and the terrible beauty of the sight, experienced too soon the elation of his first victory. The S-boat skippers, the elite of the Kreigsmarine and fanatical young National Socialists to a man, were not going to abandon their stricken comrade just like that. Two of the lean, white-painted craft broke away from the rest of the pack. They swung round and raced towards the *Rose*, hulls high in the air, one to port and one to starboard.

'*Change turrets!*' Gowan the Guns yelled fervently, as the S-boats' 20-mm cannon commenced chattering and a stream of multi-coloured tracer shells hissed low across the sea towards the *Rose*. His gunners took the challenge up swiftly, sweating profusely, as they raced the turrets round and spun their wheels with desperate haste. But they had not reckoned with the more experienced Germans' sudden tactic. Twin lights blazed on both the wildly swaying ships like two pairs of malevolent eyes being opened. They caught the bridge in their intense light, pinning it down from both sides like a struggling fly trapped on a collector's card. Dazzled, the *Rose* steered blindly towards them, the men on the bridge seeming to burn in the brilliant light, their arms held in front of their eyes in vain. For what seemed an age they ran forward at thirty knots on what could only be a collision course. Nobody spoke. Nobody moved. They were only five hundred yards apart.

Suddenly and surprisingly it was Pollacks who acted first. With a curse, he sprang forward. One swift grunt and he had elbowed the paralysed young helmsman to one side. He swung the wheel hard to port. In a flash the others were sent staggering to the other side of the bridge and the spell was broken. As the *Rose* heeled over, her plates screeching in protest at the violent manoeuvre, the lights vanished and they could see again.

'Good work,' cried Lamb. 'Now back to starboard again!'

But Pollacks did not appear to hear. His eyes were wide and staring, his face almost green with fear and his breath rasping.

Pollacks had not wanted to manoeuvre – he had wanted to escape.

'Doan,' Lamb yelled desperately, 'get on that wheel – for Christ's sake!'

But it was already too late to avert the imminent tragedy. As Doan sprang forward and wrenched the wheel from Pollacks's nerveless hands, the two S-boats broke off their attack. Summoned by the urgently flickering Aldis Lamp of their flotilla leader to join the assault on a much juicier prize, they surged forward at an impossible speed towards the unsuspecting and tightly bunched Ds, now emerging from the dawn mist into the trap that Wilhelmshaven had planned for them two days before.

The sea was alive with torpedoes. Just as the *Defiance's* lookout yelled his frantic warning, they hissed through the water, evil arrow-heads of impending doom. *Five ... six ... seven ... ten.* Yorke, clutching on to his bridge as the *Defiance* heeled crazily back and forth, gave up counting as the German torpedoes fanned out to port and starboard to embrace his whole flotilla, caught so completely off guard as it had begun to slow down to rendezvous with HMS *Rose*.

His captains reacted brilliantly. Giving his own ship maximum rudder so that the *Defiance* heeled over violently, Yorke saw two torpedoes hiss past the stern a boat's length away. *Destruction,* impeccably handled by O'Brien, weaved in miraculously between three torpedoes.

Collins of the *Daring* was not so lucky. Perhaps he had concentrated too much on bringing his guns into action and neglected the torpedoes hurrying towards him. At any rate he died in the same instant that the first torpedo struck his ship with the reverberating echo of metal striking metal. The second struck the *Daring* amidships. For a moment nothing seemed to happen. Then, from deep down inside the destroyer, there was a muffled explosion, followed by the ear-splitting scream of high-pressure steam escaping.

Flame spurted a hundred feet into the air, illuminating all around it with the searing clarity of a photographer's flash, in a picture that Yorke would never forget until the day he died: fear-crazed men on fire, beating insanely at their burning uniforms with hands rapidly being transformed into blackened claws; men sprawled out in pools of greedy blue flame tinged with oily smoke; on the paint-bubbling deck, their backs arched in death; men with faces inhumanly contorted flinging themselves over the side, burning fiercely like torches in a sea that itself was already aflame, and thrashing there in unspeakable agony until the flames consumed them. Not a few men, but scores of them, screaming soundlessly as they died in anguish.

A mere moment later, or so it seemed to a sickened Yorke, the *Daring* exploded. When the smoke vanished he saw the lean white killers skimming back the way they had come at forty knots, racing callously through the bobbing heads of the few survivors, and on past a stationary HMS *Rose* apparently sheltering in a little cove, almost as if she were trying to keep out of the way, her six five-inch guns strangely silent.

THREE

Captain Vernon Yorke looked old, his face grey, haggard and blotched, as he reported the *Daring's* casualties to his assembled captains in the *Defiance's* wardroom, 'One hundred and fifty drowned, ten wounded or burnt and forty unwounded rescued.' He hesitated a fraction of second. 'I'm afraid that poor Commander Collins was not picked up among the survivors.'

As he listened to the Flotilla Captain's words, delivered in a matter-of-fact manner, Lamb writhed in an agony of spirit and knew the sour taste of self-loathing. The Germans had tricked him, outfought him, and he had failed to realise in advance what a coward his First Officer really was. He should have kicked Pollacks off the bridge right from the beginning. Due indirectly to his lack of foresight, one hundred and fifty British sailors had gone to their deaths.

'It is a very sad business,' Yorke was saying huskily. 'Collins was a good officer, I shall miss him. He deserved a better fate than that, caught without a real chance of fighting back... All the same, there is one slight consolation, he is with the Lord now,

118

knowing that he has done his duty. And now, gentlemen, we must concern ourselves with the future. The reason I have called you from your ships is to inform you that the Admiralty has signalled that we shall not be returning to Scapa as originally planned after laying the mines. We are to steam on a northerly course heading for Norwegian waters. You see, according to NI*, the Boche invasion of that country is now only a matter of hours away.

'The signal I received an hour ago, orders us to stand by to cover the landing of a British infantry brigade which is already loading in Scottish ports, planned to go ashore in the Narvik area as soon as Norway is at war. For the time being, therefore, we'll have to look after the casualties as best we can. The sickbay tiffies are fairly competent, I'm told.' He paused for a moment. 'Though I doubt they'll be able to do very much for the burn cases.'

Lamb felt a shiver of sick horror run through him at the thought of those badly burned survivors of the *Daring*, scorched black by the flames, their flesh hanging off the gleaming white bones like rags.

'No matter, it can't be helped,' Yorke continued. 'From now onwards, we shall observe strict W/T silence. All communication will be made by signal flag and Aldis.

*Naval Intelligence.

In addition, I want an intense air and radar watch to be executed. Obviously the Boche, knowing our last position, will be making educated guesses about our present one. So we must be doubly on our guard. Finally, I want you all to put your crews on action stations till I tell you to stand them down. I want no more tragedies such as the one we experienced this morning. Clear?'

The assembled captains cleared their throats and answered in the affirmative.

'All right, gentlemen, that is all. You may return to your ships now.'

There was a scraping of chairs and a shuffle of feet as the officers began to make for the door. But Captain Yorke raised his hand suddenly, as he spotted Lamb following the rest. 'Not you, Commander Lamb,' he snapped. 'Would you please remain behind? I would like to speak to you privately for a moment.'

Lamb slumped back into his chair and waited until the rest had gone.

Yorke rose and closed the door behind the last captain. Then he swung round and standing there, haggard and worn, his face was a harsh mask as he snapped, 'Commander Lamb, what explanation do you have for the failure of your ship to have participated effectively in the action with the Boche this morning?' His single eye burned into the face of the younger man.

Miserable at the thought of the sinking of the *Daring*, Lamb was not quite aware of the full implications of Captain Yorke's sudden statement. 'Well, sir for most of the night the *Rose* was crippled by engine failure. We'd just got the fault cleared up, when the German S-boats appeared without warning. Then we tackled them as best we could.'

'Not very effectively, it would appear, Commander. But I am not talking about what happened *prior* to our appearance, that is your story.' His contempt was obvious. 'I am concerned with the events *after* Commander Collins's ship was sunk.'

'What do you mean, sir?'

'I mean,' Yorke said deliberately, staring at the younger officer in naked disgust, 'why didn't you attack the S-boats after you had seen your comrade sunk in such a terrible manner? At that range, you could have hit at least one of the Boche with those five inchers of yours, safely, without any risk to your–'

'Sir,' Lamb interrupted, suddenly aware of what Yorke was implying, yet somehow unable to justify himself by explaining how Pollacks had cracked up at the crucial moment. 'The Germans had blinded us with their searchlights – a couple of them. It was a completely new trick for me. By the time we had broken away and could see again, it was already too late. The damage had been done.'

'A convenient excuse, don't you think, Lamb?'

Lamb flushed hotly. 'I resent that, sir – I resent it very much. If you don't believe me, then I would request you to question my officers. You have my permission to do so.'

Yorke laughed drily. 'Your officers,' he sneered. 'A first officer whose main interest in life seems to be womanising, a Colonial of dubious origin and two subs, who are still wet behind the ears, from *King Alfred*. What would *they* be able to tell me? No, Lamb, I'm afraid I can't buy that explanation. You see,' he hesitated, his hand touching the patch covering his missing left eye thoughtfully, 'your excuse seems to me to be reminiscent of another one given by a member of your family a long time ago.'

Lamb sat upright suddenly. For the first time that day, he flung off the mood of despair which had afflicted him ever since the sinking of the *Daring*. 'What exactly do you mean by that?'

'You are Vice-Admiral Horatio Lamb's son aren't you?' Yorke asked coldly. 'Isn't that explanation enough?'

Lamb's eyes flashed fire. 'No it isn't!' he retorted. 'Besides, it is damnably unfair and you know it.'

'*Unfair*,' Yorke snapped, losing his hard-faced composure. 'What do you know about such things? I was a midshipman on the *Scarborough!*'

The name of the light cruiser sunk nearly a quarter of a century before struck Lamb almost physically. He groaned aloud, 'No, not you...'

'Yes, Commander Lamb,' Yorke replied, his voice cold, 'I was one of the three survivors of the *Scarborough!*'

'It is for that reason, and what happened this morning in the Strait, Commander Lamb, that I am recommending you for a court-martial as soon as we return to port. The charge will be cowardice in the face of the enemy.'

Although it was only four in the afternoon, Sub-Lieutenant Doan was sprawled in one of the wardroom's scuffed leather arm-chairs, drinking a large pink gin when Lamb entered. For a moment he attempted to hide his glass, but when he saw the shocked look on Lamb's face, the fact that he was drinking so early in the day didn't seem to matter any more.

'What's the matter, skipper? Has old Popeye been giving you a hard time?'

Lamb's eyes focused on the pink gin. 'Get me one of those – a double, Doan, if you would. I need it.'

'Sure, skipper.' His face puzzled, Doan

rose and pressed the bell for the steward.

A couple of minutes later, the colour returning to his pale cheeks after a deep draught of the gin, Lamb made his announcement. 'I'm to remain in charge of the *Rose* until we return to port after this Norwegian business, then I'm for the law.'

'The law?'

'Yes, Captain Yorke has just informed me that I am to be court-martialled on account of that business this morning. The charge is cowardice in the face of the enemy.' He took a deep drink of the powerful spirit.

'Aw, you must be kidding, skipper!' Doan protested. 'Hell, didn't we sink one of the Heinie bastards? What's wrong with Yorke – is he losing his marbles or something? *Cowardice!*' He snorted contemptuously. 'The only guy on this ship who is a coward is that chicken-shit Mr Pollacks – and I'll go and testify that to any court in the land.'

Lamb smiled sadly. 'Thank you, Doan. But you see it goes deeper than that.'

'What do you mean, skipper?'

'I am the son of Vice-Admiral Lamb and my dead father has – er, a certain reputation among the older officers in the Royal Navy.'

'I don't follow you, skipper.'

'Well in 1916 my father was the youngest admiral in the Royal Navy. He had done well in the China Sea and off South Africa and he had gone up the ladder of promotion prettily rapidly for those days. In 1907 they had promoted him captain and given him one of the first Dreadnoughts, which naturally didn't please a lot of people, especially as a lot of officers senior in service to him were passed over. So he had enemies.'

Doan nodded his understanding. 'Yeah, it's the same old story the world over.'

'Well, as I was saying, he was a vice-admiral in 1916 when Beatty gave him command of the Third Heavy Cruiser Squadron just two months before Jutland. Again a lot of people were angry. They said he was too young for the command, he had powerful friends at court, that sort of thing. In essence there were those who expected him to fail and were prepared to pillory him when he did. They got their chance.' He nodded to Doan. 'Ring for the steward. We'll have another gin, eh? I damn well need it today.'

Impatiently Doan waited till the elderly steward had brought the pink gins and vanished. 'Well, go on, skipper.'

Lamb smiled. 'Half way through the Battle of Jutland, the German Dreadnoughts, *Koeln*, *Koblenz* and *Kassel* managed to break through the destroyer screen protecting the Grand Fleet. At that stage of the fight, everything had become very confused. But one thing was certain. The German guns and armour were far superior to the British. It was imperative, therefore, to keep the German Dreadnoughts from getting too close to the British battleships. The destroyers had failed. Now it was the turn of the Second Light-Cruiser Squadron. Naturally its commander knew his ships were hopelessly outgunned by the enemy, but he accepted his orders in the true Nelson fashion and with the promise that Admiral Lamb's Heavy Cruiser Squadron was coming to his assistance at top speed. If he could hold up the enemy for a matter of an hour, Lamb's ships with their new eight-inch guns would help him out of the mess that was expected to develop.' He paused and took a drink. 'The Second went in and started firing at the German Dreadnoughts with their pathetic little guns at, say, five thousand yards. I suppose the Germans must have felt like an elephant being stung by a horsefly for all the damage the British shells did. Naturally they closed swiftly, eager to get at the Grand Fleet, and really plastered the Second. The Squadron Commander stuck it out – he must have been a very brave man, then he could have made smoke and run for it, relying on his much superior speed to get out of the range of the German guns. But he knew what was at stake and naturally he was relying on my father's ships to appear at any moment. So he stayed and fought, waiting desperately for the Third Heavy Cruiser Squadron to turn up and save him.'

Lamb drained his glass bitterly to the dregs. 'But Admiral Lamb did not appear, and one by one, the Germans blasted the light cruisers out of the water, as if they were made of paper and not best British steel. In all there were three survivors who were picked up – the Germans had no time to pick up the rest. One of those three was Captain Vernon Yorke.' He put down his empty glass on the table with an air of finality.

'But what had happened to your father, skipper? Why hadn't he turned up?'

'The excuse – if that's what you call it – he gave at the trial was that his flagship HMS *Attack* had developed boiler trouble as the Squadron sailed to the assistance of the light cruisers. His engine room had assured him that it would take only a mere half hour to solve the problem and not knowing how desperate the light cruisers' situation was my father had ordered the whole Squadron to wait.'

'But why didn't he transfer his flag to one of his other cruisers?' Doan objected.

'Exactly! That was just what the court asked at the trial. Why hadn't he left his flagship to solve its problems and follow at its own pace. But you see, Doan,' Lamb said, eagerly leaning forward to convince the American, 'they were trying my father after the war, in 1918. And by that time people's attitudes had changed. There had been a lot of action and a lot of death since Jutland two years before. People had grown cynical, war weary, concerned with looking after their own skins. They simply could not understand my father's old-fashioned attitude that big men deserved the glory of battle after sitting on their bottoms for two years in Scapa Flow. As he saw it, he couldn't abandon them when at last they had this golden opportunity to tackle the Hun, as my father used to call the Germans. Do you understand?'

Doan shrugged non-committally, and Lamb gave him a half smile. 'I can see you don't. The court didn't either. I'm sure they laughed behind my father's back when he made statements like that. The result was that he was found guilty of cowardice, stripped of his rank – they even took back his decorations – and dismissed him from the service.' Lamb shrugged. 'And that was that.'

'What happened then?' Doan asked softly.

'Not much. My father tried to rehabilitate himself. When I was home from school during the holidays, I can remember him sitting in his study for hours on end, talking to himself and writing letter after letter to

128

important people, which were never answered, or standing on the edge of the Sound, watching the naval craft go by through his telescope, his face filled with–' he sought momentarily for the right word – 'with, I suppose you could call it longing. In the end he gave in. His heart was broken and he knew there was no further hope. When I was twelve, he got up just before seven in the morning, dressed up in his old uniform, with the patches where his badges of rank and decorations had been, and ... and blew out his brains.'

'*Christ*,' Doan whispered. 'Christ on a crutch! What is Yorke trying to do then, victimise you, eh?'

Lamb shrugged. 'Maybe, but what does it matter with my background? All I know is that when Lieutenant-Commander John Lamb, DSC, gets back to port after this little do is over, he's for the high jump.'

FOUR: *IN THE WESTFJORD*

'By the time Captain Yorke finds out, he'll be writing up his recommendation for our gongs – or those nice little sad letters to our next-of-kins.'

Lieutenant-Commander Lamb
to Sub-Lieutenant Doan,
April 10th 1940.

ONE

Late on the afternoon of Sunday April 7th, Commander Roope, the captain of HMS *Glowworm*, was informed that she had lost a man overboard. He immediately signalled his flotilla commander, Captain Warburton-Lee, requesting permission to turn about and search for the missing rating. He received that permission, and leaving the destroyer flotilla heading for the mine-laying operation in the Westfjord, began his search. It proved fruitless but, just as he decided to give up and join the rest of the flotilla, the weather began to thicken and as Monday had dawned, overcast and foggy, the H-class destroyer found herself alone in the middle of the tossing, glass-green sea.

By midday the wind was howling across the water at gale force, buffeting the lone ship and making her take so much water that Roope ordered her to reduce speed. During the early afternoon her gyro-compass broke down and the *Glowworm* had to steer by means of the magnetic compass. Thus, as the day wore on, her chances of catching up with the rest by nightfall grew slimmer and slimmer.

In the later afternoon, the second-in-command Lieutenant Ramsay, muffled in a duffle-coat on the freezingly cold bridge, had just begun to warm his icy hands on a mug of tea when down below on the swaying, streaming deck, the look-out shouted: 'Ship on the starboard bow!' Ramsay focused his glasses, balancing himself as best he could and tried to identify the long grey shape which had suddenly emerged from a fog-bank. She was a warship all right, but definitely not British.

For a moment or two he sucked his teeth thoughtfully, wondering whether he should call the Captain back to the bridge from below. The strange warship started to run up the yellow and blue Swedish flag. 'Swedish, my arse!' he cursed to no one in particular. 'She's no more Swedish than–'

He never finished his sentence. Shells ripped the air apart. One after another, they fell in the water a hundred yards away, red-hot metal hissing through the fog, sending the *Glowworm* reeling, as the urgent summons to action stations echoed and re-echoed through the destroyer.

Glowworm's guns thundered minutes later. Her gunners were more accurate than those of the unknown ship. Yellow flame spurted upwards as they slammed their shells into their target, followed instants later by a thick cloud of oily smoke, as the damaged vessel hurriedly retreated into the fogbank from which she had emerged, her guns silent.

But as a ragged cheer rose from the men on the deck below and the PA system allowed Vera Lynn to insist once again in her shrill nasal that 'we'll meet agen, don't know where, don't know when', a worried Commander Roope felt somehow that the action wasn't over for that day. There was more to come.

A quarter of an hour later, a huge shape slid from the fogbank, towering high above the 2,000-ton destroyer, followed by yet another giant and this time there was not the slightest hesitation on the *Glowworm's* bridge about the strangers' identity.

'Here come the big brothers,' Roope announced as calmly as he could. *'Hipper,* and if I'm not mistaken, the *Braunschweig.'*

Ramsay whistled softly through his front teeth. 'Both ten thousand tons with eight-inch guns.'

'Right in one,' Roope agreed, as the two giants began to turn their guns on the pitching, heaving destroyer. 'All right, signaller, make an immediate signal to Admiralty. We've spotted the Boche invasion fleet for Norway. Latitude–'

His words were drowned by the first, tremendous eight-inch gun salvo, which started as a breathless hush and developed into an all-consuming roar which swamped them a second later as the little destroyer reeled back from the impact. A huge flash blinded the officers on the bridge. The stern sagged and tons of angry water were sweeping furiously into the tremendous ragged hole which had suddenly appeared there.

'Zig-zag!' Lieutenant Ramsay gasped urgently, recovering first from the shock. 'Zig-zag, I say!'

The helmsman swung the wheel round hard. Not a moment too soon. The heavy cruisers' salvo thundered down harmlessly, missing the stricken destroyer by yards, drenching her in water. Roope, holding on grimly to the bridge as the ship swayed back and forth, barked: 'Stand by torpedo tubes, we're going in to the attack!'

Down below, the torpedo officer's voice came up the tube as calm and as detached as if this were a training exercise and not a deliberate act of suicide, 'Ay, ay, sir! Torpedo tubes standing by.'

Roope licked suddenly dry lips and took a quick glance around the bridge at the men he knew he would never see again. Then he made his decision: 'All right, Number One, stand by for torpedo approach.' He grinned suddenly. 'All aboard for the *Skylark*, Number One, eh!'

'All aboard for the *Skylark*,' Lieutenant Ramsay replied as the stricken little destroyer swung round and began to limp painfully to her doom...*

As the *Glowworm's* radio telegraphist died, trapped in his shack with the water bubbling frighteningly all around him, the steel spar mercifully penetrating his heart at once when the bulkhead gave way, the specialist ratings at the Directorate of Naval Operations were already decoding his coded garbled messages. They weren't much, but they were enough to be forwarded immediately to the ex-City gents who now staffed Room 39 at the Admiralty. *'Am attacking ... am under fire from enemy cruiser, am on fire bridge and amidships'*, thoughtfully the Intelligence men sifted through the terse, urgent messages, which revealed so little of the last agonies of those men now settling down at the bottom of the North Sea, *'Hit again, am now sinking...'*

'Well?' Geoffrey demanded of them. 'Is it the Hun invasion fleet or not?'

The Wavy Navy officers hesitated. A wrong decision now and they might have the whole of the Home Fleet heading for a secondary target while the German invasion fleet steamed unharmed towards its objective.

*The *Glowworm* succeeded in ramming the *Hipper* before she went down, taking Commander Roope and 117 men with her. Commander Roope was awarded the VC posthumously.

'What has air to report?' Lieutenant-Commander Ian Fleming asked, taking out the silver cigarette case presented to him by one of his titled female admirers, and lighting yet another Moreland Three-Ringed Special.

The Squadron Leader, who was Air Intelligence's representative, shook his head, 'Negative. We've got planes up all over the area. But so far none of them has reported a sausage. The weather, apparently, is shocking off the coast of Norway. Visibility is now down to zero. Most of them will be lucky if they make it back to base.'

Thus that tense, confused April 8th wore on, while at the Admiralty they waited for the confirmation of their fears that the Germans were about to invade Norway. Just before afternoon tea, British Intelligence's Government Communication Centre, hidden at its remote country headquarters at Bletchley and known to its members as the 'Golf and Chess Club', picked up a message transmitted by the German top secret coding machine Enigma. The Bletchley experts had not yet completely broken all Enigma's secrets, but they made sufficient sense of the high priority message to forward it to Naval Intelligence in London.

'*Hipper* ... suffered ... returning port... Proceeding course... Dietl wishes *Bergheil*...'

'Well?' Godfrey asked, taking his eyes off

the sheer black stockings of the pretty young Wren who was leaning delightfully and provocatively over the table opposite, removing the tea things, 'what do you make of it, gentlemen?'

'Well, sir,' one of them replied, 'it's pretty obvious that there is a link between the cruiser the *Glowworm* reported here,' he pointed to the coast of Norway just off Trondheim on the big map which covered the whole wall, 'and the fact that *Hipper* is returning to port. My conclusion is that she has suffered damage.'

'Yes,' Godfrey said thoughtfully, 'I'll buy that. But the question still remains – is this the invasion fleet?' The tension broke through suddenly. 'We can't go on procrastinating much longer. Winnie will be breathing down our necks for information any moment now!'

'For my money, sir,' Commander Fleming's cool drawl broke into the heavy silence which had followed Admiral Godfrey's words, 'it's the invasion fleet all right.'

'What makes you so sure, Ian?'

'The last bit, sir,' Fleming answered easily, drawing at his ivory cigarette holder.

'You mean "Dietl wishes – er – *Bergheil?*"'

'Yessir.'

'Well, get on with it, Ian,' Godfrey snorted, his plump face flushing a little. 'Don't try to be so damned clever!'

'Well, *Bergheil* is a greeting used by Bavarian mountaineers and skiers when they meet each other in the mountains of that part of the world.' Carefully Fleming lit another hand-made cigarette from the stub of the one in his holder. 'So the question for me was who is Dietl... It didn't take me long to find out. He is General-Major Dietl, Commanding General of the Third German Mountain Division, a man in other words who would use a greeting of that kind. Perhaps to his corps commander, General von Falkenhorst. So, suddenly we find our tired but presumably happy skiers from Hamburg's red-light district transferred to yet another highly unlikely locale off the coast of Norway, being very seasick and we conclude—'

'We conclude,' Admiral Godfrey interrupted excitedly, 'that the combination of naval vessels and a mountain division commander indicates that this is the invasion force bound for Northern Norway! *Ian, get me the First Lord...*'

Just before dusk the signals started to flash out from the Directorate of Naval Operations in London to naval and Fleet Air Arm units the length and breadth of the United Kingdom – to the infantry brigade already sailing from the Scottish ports, to Captain Warburton-Lee's destroyer flotilla already positioned off Narvik – and finally

140

Captain Yorke's Eighth Destroyer Flotilla, steaming steadily northwards in weather that was deteriorating by the minute.

'*DNO to Capt Commanding 8th D.F.*' the message read in its impersonal officialese. '*Enemy reported vicinity Trondheim/Narvik. Rumoured already landing troops. 8th D.F. will proceed all speed to join Warburton-Lee for further instructions. Good luck!*'

One hour later, as HMS *Rose* pitched violently in the swift-running sea and the first icy flurries of snow began to descend upon the little flotilla dwarfed by the huge waves, Commander Lamb addressed his shivering crew over the PA system and told them of the new plan. 'I have been informed by the Flotilla Commander that we shall be going into action again in the immediate future. According to our Intelligence, the Jerries are landing troops, – or will be soon – in the Trondheim-Narvik area. We shall be doing the same as soon as infantry arrives from the UK. In the meantime we are to join the Second Destroyer Flotilla under a Captain Warburton-Lee. According to Captain Yorke it will be probably our job to clear any Jerry naval craft out of the fjords up there so that our boys can land without trouble, and capture the vital ore port of Narvik.' Lamb paused for a moment and the crew, heads tucked into duffle coats on the icy deck, sprawled in their hammocks below, or trying desperately to keep their balance in the galley as they prepared the evening meal, could hear him breathe out in a harsh metallic rasp over the PA system. 'I don't know quite how to put this, chaps. But the *Rose* didn't put up too good a show in the Skaggerak action. The Flotilla Commander thinks we can do better and perhaps he's right. At all events, chaps,' he concluded a little helplessly, as if he were confused himself and didn't quite believe what he was saying, 'I want each and every one of you to pull his weight when we meet the Jerry again and pay him back for what he did to the poor old *Daring*. That's all.'

As Scouse, dragging his hammock from the rack and slinging it directly beneath the coveted hot-air louver, commented sadly a little while later: 'The skipper's on his uppers, lads. You could tell that from his voice, the unlucky sod.' Expertly he tied the hammock up while the green hands clustered around him enviously holding up their frozen hands to the heat streaming from the vent. 'So you young uns, who still believe in fairies at the bottom of the garden, cubs' honour and peace-in-our-time (especially you Paddy fisheaters) better start going on yer knobbly knees and praying that the bloody old *Rose* don't go and bugger up things for him agen.'

TWO

Captain Warburton-Lee, a square-faced officer with his hair parted neatly down the centre of his head in the fashion of the twenties, stared at Captain Yorke across the *Hardy's* wardroom. 'All right, Vernon, I suggest we get down to business at once.

'The Boche are in,' he waved a hand vaguely in the direction of Westfjord, which lay two miles off the *Hardy's* port bow. 'They've beat us to it and I should imagine they're already landing troops.'

'I see. What is the Boche strength?'

'I don't know for certain, Vernon, of course. But my guess is ten destroyers.'

'And the heavy cruiser reported in the *Glowworm* action?'

'She's not present. Probably she's returned to Bremerhaven or some other German harbour.'

Yorke's face brightened a little. 'So it looks as though we're fairly evenly matched with your five, and my four destroyers, eh?'

'Yes, but I'm not going to overplay my hand, Vernon,' Warburton-Lee said sombrely. 'We'll have to have reserves when our own troops land. Once the big boys are forced to

SITUATION OFF NARVIK, APRIL 1940

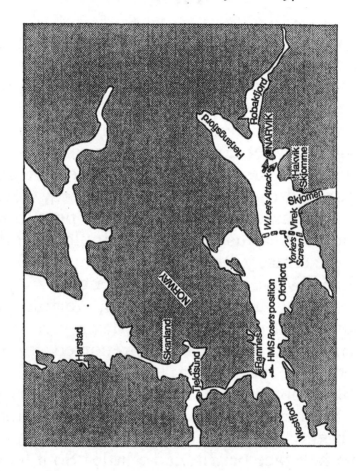

leave them at the entrance to the fjord, those troopers will be sitting ducks for any Boche destroyer that can get through to them.'

'Naturally, I agree. So what is your plan?' Yorke flashed an anxious glance through the porthole. The snow was coming down in thick, wet flakes, as if it would never stop again. 'I don't like the look of that weather out there. Under these conditions it's going to be pretty tricky in the fjord.'

Warburton-Lee nodded grimly; he knew full well that the long fjord leading up to the vital iron-ore town of Narvik was difficult to navigate at the best of times, but in such weather conditions and with possible enemy interference it would be a very hairy proposition indeed. 'I intend to go in with my own flotilla with my flagship, the *Hardy,* in the lead. My navigation officer is a first rate man and I have full confidence in his ability to get us up the fjord. Once in, I shall attack and destroy all German shipping off Narvik. You will follow, Vernon, with your flotilla and take care of any Boche that might possibly slip through us. At the same time, you will land small naval parties at Hakvik, Skjommes and Virek, here, here and here, and secure the area for our infantry.

'I also want you to station one of your ships off Ramnes here, ordering her captain to land a small party to secure the place. I know what the captain in question will say to the assignment, at least behind your back. But I need someone up there as a sort of backstop position to keep us informed in case the Boche does try to run in some strength, though I think that is highly unlikely. With the *Hipper* on her way back to the Fatherland, he's got nothing out here that could frighten us, what, Vernon?'

Captain Yorke did not altogether like his new assignment; it placed his flotilla definitely in the second team. But Warburton-Lee was his senior on the Navy List and he had to obey his orders.

'By the way,' Warburton-Lee queried casually, as they shook hands and prepared to go their respective ways, 'Who are you going to give the Ramnes assignment to?'

Captain Yorke did not hesitate. 'The *Rose,* commanded by Lieutenant-Commander Lamb, son of *the* Lamb.'

A bad omen, was the first thought that flashed into Warburton-Lee's mind. But he did not express it. Instead he contented himself with, 'Oh, well, Vernon, I'm sure he'll turn out all right.'

As Warburton-Lee's brave little force sailed directly for Narvik, the wind slashed the snow and sleet cruelly against the look-outs' purple, narrow-eyed faces. The destroyers' tripods and rigging were white glistening Christmas trees of frost and ice, while the swaying decks were heavy in ankle-deep slush. But the sailors, huddled at the guns in this strange, new, silent world of whirling snowflakes, were vital and alert. For now they knew that their ships, steaming silently down the fjord like grey ghosts, were within range of the unsuspecting German destroyers anchored within the Norwegian harbour.

Suddenly, unexpectedly, the snowstorm cleared for a fleeting instant. It was long enough for Warburton-Lee, standing tensely on the freezing open bridge, his eyes narrowed to slits, to spot the first enemy vessel. 'There she is, Stanning!' he yelled exuberantly to the Paymaster-Lieutenant, his secretary. 'A Boche destroyer!' He swung round to the helmsman, 'Hard aport,' he ordered. 'Stand by torpedoes. *Fire!*'

The first torpedo slid clumsily into the water with a slight hiss as it charged itself. '*One ... two .. three ... four,*' anxiously Warburton-Lee counted off the minutes under his breath, as the two-ton killer closed in on its target. There was a thick throaty crump. The enemy destroyer heeled over violently. 'We've hit the bugger!' Stanning yelled madly.

Warburton-Lee's eyes gleamed. First score to them, he told himself, and ordered the rest of his ships to pick targets of opportunity and begin firing. They needed no urging. *Hunter,* twisting and turning to get

147

out of the *Hardy's* wake, fired its first torpedo. It struck a fully laden ore ship directly amidships. The merchantman broke in half and went down within seconds. On the *Hardy's* deck, the frozen yet excited seamen raised a hoarse cheer.

'Look out down below!' a signaller shouted from the crow's nest, 'torpedo on the port bow!'

'*Hard over!*' the *Hardy's* Captain reacted at once.

The German torpedo streaked viciously past the destroyer with only feet to spare. Crashing into the beach beyond at fifty knots, it exploded with a roar, throwing shingle and sand high into the air.

Now the *Hardy* was plunging deep into Narvik harbour, writhing wildly from side to side, as he dodged torpedo after torpedo. On the madly swaying bridge, Paymaster-Lieutenant Stanning hung on for dear life, dabbing his brow with the dirty blue handkerchief held in his free hand, and wondering why the devil he had deserted his cabin to help out on the bridge.

'All right now,' Warburton-Lee made his quick decision, as the first startled German gunners began to open up erratically from the shore, 'I think we've done all we can do here, Stanning. Let's get away westwards.'

Ten minutes later, as they had just cleared the harbour entrance without a single casualty, three lean grey shapes loomed up out of the driving snow. 'Cruisers!' Warburton-Lee cried. 'We're not getting involved with those gentlemen. Full ahead!'

The little flotilla increased its speed to thirty knots, smoke streaming from their rakish funnels, white waves curling back from their bows. But the Germans reacted quicker than Warburton-Lee had anticipated. Their 12.7 cm guns erupted with a flash of ugly red and yellow flame. At 3,000 yards they could hardly miss. With a frenzied unnerving screech, the German shells hissed flatly across the fjord.

The *Hardy* reeled violently as a shell struck her bridge. Groggily, Stanning pulled himself to his feet. All three ratings were dead. He staggered over to the Navigation Officer, Lieutenant Smith. 'Are you all right, Gordon?' he gasped.

Smith's eyes flickered open for a brief moment; then the whites rolled upwards and his head slipped to one side. He was dead. Stanning wiped the scum from his lips with the back of his hand, and bent over the Captain.

Warburton-Lee was dying. His uniform was in rags, and blood was pouring down his face, spurting in a thick jet from a deep wound in his side. 'Captain … Captain Warburton-Lee,' he called desperately.

The Captain looked up at him. 'I've had it,

149

Stanning. If the ship's finished, give orders … to abandon… Give the chaps a chance.'

The Paymaster-Lieutenant, who, when he volunteered to come on the bridge, had not imagined that he would soon be commanding the ship, flung a quick glance around him. The *Havock* was desperately trying to lay a protective smoke-screen around the crippled, helpless *Hotspur* and a fiercely burning *Hunter.* He could expect no help from them. He would have to manage by himself as best he could. Abandoning the shattered bridge, he doubled down to the wheelhouse.

The rating in charge hung lifelessly over his wheel. Hurriedly Stanning pushed him to one side and grabbed the wheel. It responded at once. The stricken ship ceased going in circles, but just as a somewhat surprised Stanning managed to bring the *Hardy* under control, he sensed that the engines were beginning to slow down beneath him. He'd never get the *Hardy* out of the Westfjord. There was only one course open to him now – he must beach her.

'*Abandon ship!*' he called, as he began to steer the stricken destroyer towards the shore some three hundred yards away, the engines getting weaker by the second. 'And get Captain Warburton-Lee over the side – he's still alive!'

The dying Captain was quickly lowered to

a little raft, as the *Hardy* approached the high, snow-covered cliffs, with the German destroyers slamming shell after shell into the dying ship.

With a rending, metallic crash which ripped her keel open, the *Hardy* struck the pebbled beach. Flames began to leap up from her debris-littered deck. Gratefully a seriously wounded Stanning allowed himself to be lowered to the sand by two ratings. 'The Captain,' he gasped, 'did he make it?'

The older of the two shook his head slowly. 'No, sir,' he said softly, 'he died before they got him ashore.'

Captain Warburton-Lee's attack on Narvik had failed.

THREE

The bitter wind had dropped now. But the snow was still falling, steadily. Commander Lamb, fighting back a tendency to shiver, looked at his watch. It was nearly nine. Captain Warburton-Lee's force had been in action over three hours. But there had been no sound of firing from higher up the narrow fjord for an hour now. He must have completed his mission successfully. He and Yorke would probably be ensuring that the three landing spots for the infantry brigade expected within the next 24 hours were firmly in the hands of the landing parties.

Lamb gave a little sigh and wished once again that he could have gone in with the rest of the destroyers, instead of having been condemned to the dreary patrol duty. He shot a quick glance at the landing-party. Bone-chilled, frozen and pink-faced, the sailors were assembled on the poop deck under Degenhardt's hard gaze, stamping their icy feet in the powdery snow and shifting the unaccustomed rifles on their shoulders. There weren't many of them, but he could not afford any more and besides, the little Norwegian timber village, some

152

five hundred yards away across the now placid water, lay still and peaceful, as if the war had passed it by.

'Pollacks,' he turned reluctantly to the First Officer standing at his side.

'Yessir,' Pollacks voice was low and husky.

'You understand that I cannot spare another officer, Pollacks,' Lamb said carefully and slowly. 'Mr Doan has taken over your job for the time being. I don't want to send you. But you're the only officer available. You'll have to go.'

Pollacks looked up slowly. His face was very pale and there were violet rings under his lack-lustre eyes, but he had conquered the trembling of his hands. 'Doan told me about Yorke's charges, Captain,' he said hoarsely. 'I know it was my fault...' His bottom lip trembled suddenly. 'I ... I appreciate it, Captain...'

Lamb put his hand firmly on Pollacks's arm and pressed hard. 'Don't talk about it, Pollacks. You are not to blame. A captain has to take the responsibility for his men. I failed to do so.' The muscles of his jaw hardened, as the full realisation of what he was saying hit him. 'I must pay the price for that failure.'

'But sir–'

'No buts, Pollacks,' Lamb interrupted him. 'You know your mission? You'll secure the village, take the telegraph office and the

police station, confiscating any weapons –
though I'm sure you're not going to have
any trouble from the Norwegians, they're
our allies now – and then send out a small
patrol to the east. Over to that pine forest
you can see at two o'clock. Get them to dig
in and keep a weather eye for any German
troops that might be working their way to
the entrance of the fjord.'

'And you, sir?'

'We'll be patrolling about a mile off shore.
You'll maintain strict W/T silence naturally,
but I've given you Signaller Smith. As long
as this damn snow doesn't get any thicker I
should imagine we'll be able to keep in
touch in that way. All right, Pollacks, it's too
damn cold to be hanging around out here.
You'd better be on your way, and good luck.'

Pollacks bit his lip and dropped his eyes.
'Thank you, sir.'

Behind them, Degenhardt bellowed: 'All
right, you lucky men, let's be having yer!
Over the side now and woe betide any man
who drops his bondhook in the hogwash.★
Come on now – move it!'

'All right, me lucky lads!' Degenhardt
commanded as the snow fell in steady wet
flakes, 'put yer backs into it. *In ... out ... in ...
out...* Come on, move them oars now!'

★Rifle in the water.

'Bloody hell,' Scouse cursed to his mate Bunts, as the long tapering blades cut the water and sent a thin film of icy spray hissing through the air into his face. 'That Jerry bastard'll be coming down here with a cat-o'-nine tails in a mo, like that big fat sod in *Captain Blood.*'

'It's not the Coxswain what worries me, Scouse,' Bunts gasped. 'It's what we're gonna meet in that village.'

Scouse grinned. 'Snow White and the seven dwarfs, of course, yer silly sod! You're a proper old ray of sunshine, you are, Bunts. That lot in the village is our allies now. In ten minutes or so, we'll be having our feet under the table, tucking into a plate of hot grub and getting our hands under the skirt of some grateful Norwegian Judy, mark my words. We're coming as their allies, you see. Happy days is here again!'

Bunt's sole retort was a mournful, 'Bollocks!'

Now they were two hundred yards away from the little wood-built village clustered around the timber jetties that ran out into the fjord from the high-cliffed cove. Behind them the *Rose* had disappeared into the white gloom. The men straining in the longboat appeared to be alone in the silent fjord, for it seemed to Lieutenant Pollacks as he surveyed the Norwegian village through his glasses that it was deserted. There was no smoke coming from its chimneys and the single, snow-covered street was empty. 'What do you think, Coxswain?' he asked, lowering his binoculars at last.

Degenhardt tightened his pistol belt, and frowned thoughtfully. 'I don't rightly know, sir. If they'd have run away from the – er – Germans, they'd have taken their boats to my way of thinking. Then it would have been difficult to have got them up them cliffs in this weather – and with women and kids.' He indicated the steep cliffs, which hemmed in the village on all sides.

Pollacks nodded.

'But if you look over to ten o'clock, you can see that their boats are still there. So where are they?'

Pollacks rubbed his weak chin. 'Yes, where are they?'

A few moments later the longboat ground to a halt in the thick wet shingle of the little beach to the left of the village. Hastily Degenhardt and Pollacks sprang out and crunched across the pebbles, revolvers drawn, while the seamen shipped their oars and picked up their rifles. For a couple of minutes, the PO and the officer crouched as if half expecting a burst of sudden machine-gun fire from the strangely silent village. But none came and in the end, Pollacks swung round, still grasping his service revolver tightly, as if he needed to feel its comfortable weight in his fist in order to keep up his courage.

'All right, we'll proceed cautiously.' He nodded to Scouse. 'Leading Seaman, you take half a dozen men and come in from round the back of the village. Petty Officer, you and the rest follow me, we'll go in by the front door. All right, on your way, Leading Seaman!'

Cautiously, the seamen, rifles held tensely at the ready, advanced up either side of the track which led to the little village. There was no sound save the soft crunch of their nailed seaboots on the snow and the faint howl of the wind. Pollacks bit his lip to stop it trembling and told himself once again that he must control himself. He must not fail this time.

Just short of the first dark-brown timbered house, its roof heavy with a coat of snow, he halted them. 'Get down,' he ordered. 'Petty Officer.'

'Sir?'

'I'm going up to that house. You follow me at twenty paces. If,' he hesitated, 'if anything ... happens to me, you take over.'

'Sir!'

Half crouched, body tense, Pollacks eased forward, the palms of his hands wet with sweat. His boots seemed to make a terrible din crunching over the snow. Still there was no movement from the house. He could see the fish drying under the eaves and the way the snow was melting around the chimney, as if, somewhere within, a stove was still burning. Didn't that mean the house was occupied, and if it were, why had no one shown himself by now? He forced himself to go on.

'Hello?' Pollacks called, as he came round to the front of the house, his voice seeming strange and far away, 'Hello, is there anyone there, please?'

There was no answer, save for the sudden howl of the wind, sweeping in a fresh flurry of snowflakes. Pollacks staggered back as they hit him in the face. Hurriedly he pulled himself together. He knew that if he did not go forward now, he would drop his revolver and begin running in panic back to the others. He must go forward. Taking a deep breath and gripping the revolver as firmly as he could in a sweat-slippery hand, he kicked hard at the door. It flew open with surprising ease to reveal a simple kitchen filled with hand-made painted wooden furniture, the sole decoration a picture of a heavy-set man with burning eyes, obviously torn from some cheap illustrated magazine. Otherwise the place was empty. But the kettle boiling merrily on the green-tiled oven in the corner indicated that whoever had lived in the place had not been long gone.

It was the same with the second house,

and with the third. They were empty. Pollacks looked at Degenhardt and beyond the PO at the ratings. 'What in heaven's name do you make of it, Petty Officer?' he demanded.

Degenhardt tilted his steel helmet upwards and scratched the back of his shaven, scarred skull in bewilderment. 'I don't rightly know what to make of it, sir,' he said, his German accent more noticeable than usual. 'All I know is that the buggers have gone – the lot of them!'

But suddenly from the other end of the little village, the treacherous silence was broken by Scouse's well-known voice crying: 'Sir, sir, over here, we found somebody!'

Excitedly the seamen crowded into the little police post, then fell back, their chests heaving with the effort of running, to allow Pollacks and the Coxswain to pass through to where Scouse was standing, staring at the portly, heavily moustachioed Norwegian policeman who knelt beneath the simple wooden cross which decorated the wall of his office.

But his plump hands were not clasped together in prayer. They were fervent claws of agony trying to pluck out the fish-gutting knife which had been plunged deep into his uniformed chest.

Meanwhile Commander Lamb, patrolling a

mile or so off shore, had made a discovery of his own. As the *Rose* swung round in a wide arc and began steaming on an easterly course again in the direction of Narvik, the swell gave way to an almost placid sea despite the wind. For a few moments Lamb was puzzled by the change. Then he spotted the reason. The water of the fjord was gradually being covered by a thick oil slick floating from the direction of the iron-ore port. He ordered half speed and leaving the bridge under Doan's command went down to the deck himself. Curiously he looked over the side as the oil-tainted water started to bring with it the debris of war: wooden ration crates, a float, a couple of broken wooden spars, the severed ends gleaming whitely against the black water, a body.

It was already beginning to drift by, face downwards, dragging behind it a length of grey sail like some improvised shroud, when Lamb realised what it was. 'Stop engines!' he bellowed.

'Stop engines!' Doan echoed above him.

'Get a couple of ratings over here with boathooks,' Lamb ordered, as the *Rose* drifted to a stop.

Hurriedly the two ratings fished for the man floating down below. Finally they succeeded in catching their hooks in the sail. 'Heave,' commanded the older one of the two. They heaved and the body came over the side, its arms spreadeagled.

In silence, Lamb and Doan stared down at the dead seaman. He was old; his almost white hair, and the tattoos that ran up his skinny grey arm already beginning to stiffen rigidly in the cold, indicated that he had been going to sea a long time.

'Poor old bastard,' Doan said softly, 'probably some old lifer, who didn't think he'd end up like this. Thought he'd finish up with his feet on the hob and his–'

'Doan,' Lamb interrupted, his voice toneless, 'look at that tattoo on his left arm.'

'Which one, skipper?'

'The one above the anchor.'

Doan stared curiously at the fading blue crest, with some kind of motto written below it in an ornamental scroll. 'I see it, skipper, but I don't quite figure what you're getting at.'

'That tattoo is the crest of Captain Warburton-Lee's ship.' He looked down at the sodden bundle on the deck. 'This poor chap is from the *Hardy*.'

Somewhere further up the fjord Captain Yorke broke radio silence to send Lamb an urgent signal, '*2nd D.F. suffered severe casualties in action against superior German naval forces, Narvik area. Taking over command. Am unable to secure assigned landing sites under these circumstances. Imperative you hold yours, therefore… Signal approach troopers at once. Will come and escort… Under no circumstances, will you leave your station. I repeat, hold your site and station till further orders. Acknowledge immediately. Yorke.'*

Lamb handed the signal to Doan and at the same time ordered the signaller to break their own W/T silence to acknowledge it. When he had gone, he licked his lips and said slowly, 'Well, Doan, now we know, don't we?'

'Yeah, the Second bought it, I guess. What now, skipper?'

Lamb's face hardened. 'You read the message, Mr Doan; we hold this position – come hell or high water.'

FOUR

The shadow detached itself from the last of the brown-timber houses which made up the silent, abandoned coastal village. 'All right, Coxswain,' the scout whispered, 'everything seems okay... I had a butcher's as far as the end of the wood. Not a sausage.'

'What yer whispering for then?' Degenhardt asked, looking at the young rating's scared face and wondering if he could trust him.

''Cause it's a bit creepy out there,' the green hand retorted. 'The wind and the trees and everything, PO.'

'All right, don't wet yer knickers!' Degenhardt cut him short contemptuously. He swung round to the others of his little patrol, crouched against the side of the house, shivering in the cold. 'Now then, this is how we're gonna do it. Follow me at six foot intervals, bayonets fixed, with you,' he indicated Scouse and Bunts, 'bringing up the rear. And if we run into trouble, don't stand around looking like spare pricks at a wedding. Get yersen down and start firing back. All right, let's be getting on with it!'

The fir forest was dark and dank, with the

dull grey light cut out by the tightly packed trees that marched up the hillside like rank after rank of immaculate, spike-helmeted Prussian Guards. But in spite of tough going, complicated by the driving snow, the Coxswain did not take the track leading east. That would have been asking for trouble he told himself. If whoever had murdered the Norwegian policeman was somewhere in the thick wood, the track would be the obvious place to be waiting for some unsuspecting patrol. Instead he ordered the ratings into the undergrowth on both sides of the track. Within a matter of minutes the sailors were lathered in a thick sweat.

At the rear of the patrol, Bunts cursed sourly: 'Bugger this for a lark! What does that Jerry bastard think we are – a lot of ruddy goats!'

'I don't know about that,' his oppo Scouse gasped, 'but I do know – you're beginning to pong like one!'

They had almost cleared the fir wood when Degenhardt, out ten yards in front of the rest, heard the unmistakable metallic click of a rifle bolt being jerked back. He stopped dead. The rating behind him almost blundered into his tense figure. Urgently he waved his arm and the ratings flopped into the snow, hearts beating furiously, hands trembling as they flashed up their rifles.

Degenhardt poked a gnarled forefinger at his chest and mouthed the words 'going forward!'

Swiftly Degenhardt slid into the bushes, putting his feet down as carefully as he could, grateful for the wind whistling through the trees and dislodging the snow in constant flurries, muffling the sound of his approach. He stopped. Through a gap in the trees, he had caught a sudden glimpse of a group of men. Most of them were dressed in dark rough clothing of the kind worn by farmers and fishermen, and the language they were using among themselves as they crouched there at the ready, the rifles poised, was Norwegian. He gave a sigh of relief. They were friends after all. 'All right, lads,' he called in a normal voice, 'they're only Norwegians!'

The civilians, crouched at the side of the trail, swung round in alarm. A giant of a man appeared in their midst, shouting angrily in Norwegian. But it wasn't the man's size which caught Degenhardt's attention. It was the Norwegian's black uniform and the makeshift band he wore around his massive right arm. He recognized it with a thrill of alarm. It was the hooked cross of his old country – the swastika!

'Open fire, lads!' he yelled, as the civilians reacted. 'It's a trap!'

Scouse reacted first, as always. He pulled

out the pin of his sole grenade. 'Watch yer coconut, PO!' he cried and heaved it towards the civilians.

The grenade sailed through the air and exploded in the Norwegians' midst. Degenhardt caught a glimpse of their terrified faces and flung himself in the snow as the first slugs hissed through the air towards him. The battle for Ramnes had commenced.

Lieutenant Pollacks was paralysed with fear when the firing impinged on his consciousness. It was what he had been expecting ever since he had been foolish enough to accept Lamb's offer to attempt to rehabilitate himself. Of course, it would have to end like this, in violence. Suddenly he found himself shaking all over, his brow wet with grey pearls of sweat. 'Why the hell did I volunteer in the first place?' he asked himself in a paroxysm of terror.

Then with a supreme effort of will he pulled himself together. He remembered old Coates, the geography master at his grammar school, pointing at the map of the world and saying in that tired old voice of his, 'You see lads, all that red on the map is ours. A potty little island off the coast of Europe owning one fourth of the world! I suppose in a way, it's worth dying for, isn't it?'

Pollacks suddenly found himself on his

feet, bellowing at the scared-looking rating guarding the entrance to the police station: 'All right, laddie, don't just stand there. Sound the darned alarm, will you?'

'When I throw my grenade,' Degenhardt called, ignoring the hiss of the civilians' bullets striking the undergrowth all around the handful of sailors, 'I want you up on yer feet and running like hell back to the village.' He pulled out the pin. 'You,' he snapped at Scouse. 'Cover me!'

He half raised himself. '*Now*,' he screamed and threw his last grenade with all his strength. For what seemed an age the civilians watched it, petrified with fear. Then they were scattering on all sides and, as the sailors doubled back the way they had come, screaming and cursing in the crazy red chaos of the explosion.

They were less than one hundred yards away from the village now, blundering wildly through the forest, the fir branches lashing and whipping at their fear-distorted, sweat-lathered faces. Soon they would be out of the trees. The first house was clearly visible.

'*Look out, Scouse!*' Bunts screamed.

Instinctively the Leading Rating fired. The first civilian who had been kneeling in the glade waiting for them, went down as if he had been pole-axed. Degenhardt caught a glimpse of a brick-red, brutalised country face. Gasping, he brought up the brass butt of his rifle. Screaming with sudden rage, he smashed it in the Norwegian's face.

'*Du dreckschwein!*' he cried, forgetting his English. He slammed the cruel butt into the bloody mess of the man's face again. The Norwegian screamed shrilly like a woman. Then he dropped to the ground without another sound. While the rest wrestled back and forth with the remainder of the civilians, the air full of their grunts, curses, screams, the Coxswain staggered against the nearest tree, blood-stained rifle held limply in his hands, all energy drained out of him for a moment.

'*Coxswain!*' Scouse's urgent call finally penetrated his consciousness. 'Over here – quick, Coxswain!'

The PO staggered across the bodies. He could hear someone crying weakly in Norwegian, while a metal rifle-butt descended upon the bone and soft flesh of his skull with brutal persistence.

'What is it, Scouse?' he gasped, trying to rouse himself from the sudden lethargy.

'Look at yon bugger, Coxswain!' Scouse, his hand shaking a little, pointed down to what lay at the side of the dead Norwegian at his feet, sprawled out like a broken doll. 'A radio – a short-wave radio; the buggers have been in contact with somebody else,

Coxswain,' Scouse breathed out, pushing back his helmet and rubbing the puckered, wet line made by its lining across his forehead. 'What do you make of it, PO?'

Behind them the sound of the pursuit was letting louder. Degenhardt pulled himself together. 'Don't know, Scouse,' he barked. 'But destroy that radio!'

'Ay, ay, Coxswain!' Scouse raised the butt of his rifle to smash down on the clumsy set. As he did so, Degenhardt's eye fell on the scrap of paper lying in the dead Norwegian operator's hand. Swiftly he pulled it out of the lifelessly crooked fingers.

'All right,' he bellowed above the sudden ragged volley of rifle fire, 'Come on, all of yer. Fingers out, now! We're gonna make a run for the last fifty yards. *Run!*'

'Well?' Lieutenant Pollacks asked, as the first bullet smacked into the thick logs of the hut in which he had set up his headquarters, 'what do you make of it, Coxswain?' His hands shook slightly, but by keeping them dug deeply into the pockets of his tunic, he knew he could hide the signs of his fear from the wild-eyed, sweat-lathered ratings of Degenhardt's party filling the hut.

'I don't rightly know, sir,' Degenhardt answered, gingerly touching the livid weal across his right cheek. 'We were proceeding through the woods as ordered when we

169

bumped into these civvies. They were Norwegian all right, not German. But they opened fire at once. There must have been at least thirty of them, and with only seven men, I thought it best to skidaddle.'

'Of course–' Pollacks jumped as another slug slammed into the wall and chips of wood began to drift down from the roof like snow – 'you were right. But who in hell's name are they? I thought the civvies were on our side?'

'I can tell you, sir,' Scouse interrupted, looking up from where he was filling a fresh magazine from the bandolier slung around his chest. 'Perhaps you remember that photo we spotted in the first house? I recognised the dekko straight-off. It's Major Vidkun Quisling – I think that's how they pronounce it. He was a great admirer of old Adolf before the war. He started a party like him.'

Suddenly it dawned on Pollacks. 'You mean he's a … a fifth columnist like in Spain?'

'That's right,' Scouse answered cheerfully, telling himself it was always the same with officers: you had to jolly them along like a lot of bleeding snotty-nosed kids. 'I mean I'm only a poor ignorant Liverpool lad. But put that dead bobby, the picture, and them blokes in the wood together and you don't need a crystal ball to work out–'

'That they're on the side of the Jerries,'

Pollacks interrupted excitedly, his fear gone now.

'Right on, sir,' Scouse answered. 'They must have spotted the *Rose* and done a bunk until they saw how few we was. Then they thought it'd be safe enough to mix it.' He winked wickedly. 'They hadn't reckoned with the old Royal though, had they, sir?'

'It looks like you're right, MacFadden. But we've got to hold this place at all costs. The skipper is relying on us. You see they're going to use this village for landing our infantry. They'll be coming in—'

'Sir,' Degenhardt interrupted him harshly.

Pollacks spun round. 'Yes, Coxswain?'

'Here, sir.' Degenhardt smoothed out the piece of paper on the rough table in front of the officer. 'I took this off a radio operator in the woods – they had one with them,' he added swiftly. 'You see, this is a sketch of the *Rose's* last position in the fjord.'

'What?' Lieutenant Pollacks exclaimed.

Degenhardt nodded grimly. 'There's no doubt about that, sir. But there's worse.'

'What do you mean?' the officer raised his voice, as the Norwegians' bullets pattered against the hut and the rating at the window opened up with the group's sole machine-gun, a Word War One Lewis.

'Below it there's something written in German. It's not too good German, but it's understandable. It was obvious they were

171

going to send a message to somebody who only spoke German.'

'Go on,' Scouse urged, 'don't keep me in suspense, Coxswain. I'll pee myself in a minute.'

For once Petty Officer Horst Degenhardt did not give the cocky Leading Rating one of his murderous glances. Instead he said grimly, 'When you've heard what I've got to say, Scouse, you'll be doing something else than that in yer pants! Sir,' he turned to Lieutenant Pollacks again. 'The message gives the latitude and approximate course of the *Braunschweig*.'

'Oh, my holy Christ. Not the ten thousand tonner, Coxswain?'

'The same, sir.'

Pollacks licked dry lips, and hesitated before he asked his question. 'And what do you make of it, Coxswain?'

As the first burst of firing from the west indicated that the Norwegian renegades were working their way round the village, obviously intent on cutting them off from the beach where their longboat was beached, Degenhardt gave him the answer he feared. 'It means they were going to signal – no, not *going* to, but *had* already signalled *Braunschweig* to come into the fjord.'

172

FIVE

It was growing darker. To the east the land mass was becoming noticeably more vague and the snow-topped cliffs looming up from the silent fjord no longer seemed so hard and crisply outlined against the sky. Gradually the white-glistening rigging of the *Rose* was beginning to slide into the gathering gloom.

Below, the galleys were going all out to prepare the crew's evening meal and there was the jingle of tin plates, knives and forks as the hungry, chilled men began to line up for it. Lamb sniffed the air, as the cheerful smell of frying penetrated even to the bridge.

'Smells like snorkers, Doan,' he commented with a tired smile to his navigator, 'snorkers and cowboy beans – the matelot's favourite.'

Doan returned his smile. 'But not mine, skipper. Those damn beans give me the trots. Ever since we sailed I've been doing the turkey trot to the heads and back every thirty minutes or so. It sure does take it out of a feller.'

Lamb laughed sympathetically. 'Occupational hazard, Doan. It's not the beans, it's sea duty and the responsibility. I was once talking to an MO about it–' He stopped short. 'What was that?'

'What?'

Lamb cocked his head to one side, leaning out over the canvas bridge screen so that he could hear better. There it was again. There was no mistaking it. The faint snap and crackle of small-arms fire coming from the land, over to the east. He looked up at Doan, his face tense and very alert.

'Can you hear it now?'

'Yessir. Somebody firing. But who – and at what?'

'I don't know who,' Lamb snapped, striding over the bridge to the voice tube, 'but I *do* know at what – at Pollacks's landing party.' He clicked off the cap. 'Bridge here. Galley – douse fires at once!' He thrust the telegraphs home. Under their feet the destroyer trembled. 'Doan,' he commanded, 'sound action stations. We're getting back to Ramnes at once. Pollacks is in trouble.'

As the first light mortar shell landed with an obscene belch on the slope behind their hut, followed a second later by a thick throaty explosion which set the floor beneath him trembling like a live thing, Pollacks knew he had to do something soon. The Norwegian renegades had been creeping closer to the hut over the last hour, and now, with his Lewis gun gone and the gathering dusk covering their movements effectively, they had got close enough to bring their two-inch mortar into action.

The mortar fired again. The bomb exploded a mere twenty yards away in a thick spurt of red flame that blazed in front of the shattered window momentarily and set them all coughing and choking in the cloud of dust which rose from the seams between the logs. On the blood-stained floor, the rating who had been grievously wounded manning the Lewis gun fought his way to his knees in the blinding dust, his ashen face wrinkled with terror.

For a moment Pollacks felt wild fear surge through him. Then gently but firmly he pushed the man down to the floor again, with a whispered: 'It's all right, lad ... all right, now.'

'Thank you, sir ... sorry, sir,' the rating gasped weakly and allowed himself to be pushed. 'I know it's all right ... sorry.'

But Pollacks knew it was not all right. They wouldn't be able to hold the hut much longer and after what Degenhardt's men had done to the Norwegians' comrades in the forest, he had not the slightest illusion about what would happen to them if they were captured. Besides it was vital Commander Lamb be informed that the *Braunschweig* probably was on its way to the entrance to the fjord. For although the dead renegade might not have been able to send his message to the German ship before Degenhardt's party had killed him, the local telegraph office was in their hands, and it would have a short wave radio as all these isolated Norwegian villages had, in case the lines went down in the heavy winter snows. He felt it in his bones that the German heavy cruiser was steaming at top speed for Westfjord.

He had a seriously wounded man on his hands. His radio had been smashed, and for all he knew the *Rose* might not spot Bunts's signals in this darkness even if she were off the coast, as Lamb had promised him she would be. The Norwegian fire was growing more intensive by the minute; it would only take one direct hit by their mortar before they were finished for good.

Suddenly it was all quite clear what had to be done. In a strange voice that seemed to belong to someone else, he heard himself saying, 'Listen, lads, I don't think we're going to stick this one much longer. Once they stop their mortaring we'll make a run for the beach.'

He paused, but the expected protest did not come. Only Degenhardt's dark eyes flashed from his face to that of the wounded man on the floor and back again. Pollacks knew immediately what the look signified.

'Don't worry, Coxswain, I'll take care of the rating!'

Degenhardt gave him a searching glance, almost as if he were seeing him for the first time. Pollacks ignored it. The past was unimportant; all that concerned him now was the present. As for the future, he knew with the clarity of a vision as he said the next words, that there would be none for him.

'All right, this is the way we're going to do it. As far as the buggers outside are concerned there are only two exits out of this hut – and they've got both covered – the door and the window. But there's a third.' He jerked his finger upwards. 'The loft up there.'

The pale ratings followed the direction of his gaze.

'It's filled with straw and fodder they must have used for their animals, but I noticed as we approached the village that the walls of the lofts are made of alternating slots – I suppose to let the air in and dry the stuff in summer. So up we go and pull out the slots at the back of the house. It's about a seven-foot jump, but the snow's deep. Anyway we'll just have to take that chance. We lower him first,' he indicated the wounded rating. 'I'll take care of him from then onwards. The rest of you make a bolt for the shore.

Naturally they'll tumble to us sooner or later. But let's hope it's later.' He hesitated, his normally weak face a mask of fierce determination. 'Remember this though, one of you has got to get through to the *Rose* and warn the Captain. You understand?'

There was a chorus of muted 'ay, ays'.

'All right then, lads, let's get on with it.'

With a grunt, Scouse wrenched free the last plank and deposited it carefully in the straw. The stale smell of hay was dispelled by the cold, salt-laden air from outside. Pollacks tugged gently at the wounded man's arm.

'All right, move up to the hole. We're going to let you down now... Coxswain give me a hand, will you please?'

Together the three of them crawled to the gap in the planks. Outside, the sky was a velvety black with a hint of silver to the east. There was no sound save for the dry crack of a Norwegian rifle, followed by a spurt of scarlet flame. Swiftly the officer and the German lowered the wounded man as far as they could.

'All right,' Pollacks whispered, 'we're going to let go. Now!'

He and Degenhardt relinquished their hold simultaneously. The rating dropped softly into the snow with only the faintest of groans. For a moment Pollacks tensed, his heart beating like a trip-hammer. Had the enemy heard? But the rifle fire continued with the same mournful, routine persistence, as the Norwegians plucked up the courage to make their last attack.

In a sudden flash of fire a couple of dozen yards away, Pollacks caught a brief glimpse of Degenhardt's eyes. They expressed a look of both admiration and confusion. 'Do you want me to stay with–'

'No,' Pollacks cut in. 'I'll handle him by myself. Somebody's got to get through to the *Rose* and whoever that is stands a better chance without the burden of that poor chap down there.' He rolled over on to his back and whispered to the others waiting in the hay. 'Okay, move up! Time to be off.'

One by one they crawled past him, rifles in hand, sliding through the hole and dropping softly into the snow. Still the Norwegians had not noticed the lack of counter-fire from the hut. Pollacks dug Degenhardt in the arm.

'Now you, Coxswain.'

'Sir–'

'Now!' Pollacks thundered. Degenhardt went, followed an instant later by the First Lieutenant.

Pollacks pulled out his revolver attached to his body by the lanyard around his neck and slipped his free arm around the wounded rating's body. 'Are we all ready?' he hissed.

'Ay, ay, sir,' the tense answer came back, as

they crouched there in the dark shadow of the little hut.

'Good, let's not waste any more time. You take the lead, Coxswain... I'll bring up the rear. Single file. Off you go – and good luck to the lot of you, lads...'

'What the hell's going on over there, Mr Doan?' Lamb cried angrily, knowing instinctively that the *Rose* had run into trouble again, as the ugly flames split the darkness on the shore.

'God knows,' Doan replied. 'All I can tell you skipper, is that it ain't a Texas-style turkey-shoot going on on the shore. Jimmy B – excuse me, Mr Pollacks has run into trouble.'

'Oh, thank you for the kind information, Mr Doan,' Lamb sneered, beside himself with rage at the thought that the *Rose's* jinx was working again. 'I would never have guessed by myself.'

He put down his night-glasses. They revealed nothing of what was happening on the dark shore. He bit his lip for a moment and considered what he should do. Obviously Pollacks was in trouble – perhaps he had bumped into an advance force of Germans moving up from Narvik. But could he risk his ship to go in and help Pollacks? Yorke's strict orders to keep his position flashed through his mind. Would he be justified in leaving it under these circumstances? Instinctively he knew what Captain Yorke would have done. He would have abandoned the handful of men on the shore in order not to risk his ship and its crew in the tricky shoals.

'Well?' Doan demanded as a fresh burst of firing crackled from across the still dark water. 'What are you going to do, skipper?'

Lamb tugged the end of his nose. 'Naval regulations state, Lieutenant Doan, that any captain who unnecessarily places his ship in a position of danger is subject to court-martial.' He smiled coldly. 'I am going to do exactly that, Mr Doan.' He raised his voice. 'All right, Doan, stand by with another boat. We're going in as close as we dare – and put a double lookout on the bow. I don't want the *Rose's* jinx to act up on us again and to find ourselves with our bottom ripped on one of those inshore shoals.'

Doan's face lit up enthusiastically. 'May I volunteer to take in the second boat, sir? I'd like to have some – er–' He looked down at his suddenly clenched fist, 'personal contact with the Heinies.'

'You may, Doan. But remember you're not to go and get yourself killed – you're a neutral.'

The dark clouds parted in the moon's path. For an instant the beach gleamed in its cold

181

light, and the little landing party crouched in the rocks overlooking it, could see it was empty of Norwegians. Their boat, drawn up high on the wet glistening shingle, was unguarded too.

Pollacks breathed a hushed sigh of relief. Perhaps he would not have to die after all. The renegades had not yet spotted their escape from the hut.

'Coxswain,' he whispered urgently. 'Take MacFarland here and the Leading Signaller and get to the boat. Try to float her with as little noise as possible. We'll give you five minutes and then follow. I'll bring up the rear with this poor chap,' he indicated the dying gunner.

'Ay ay, sir,' Degenhardt snapped softly. 'All right, Scouse and Bunts – follow me. And one little sound from either of yer,' he warned, 'and yer'll be on the rattle before yer can say Jack Robinson. Come on!'

Pollacks watched them go, restraining the desire to break cover and run after them; he knew once they started to push the boat out, the noise it made on the shingle would soon alarm the Norwegians up above them in the now almost silent village. He saw them pause against the side of a strangely shaped rock that towered up in stark black silhouette like the steeple of a cathedral he had once seen on a visit to Barcelona. Then they were gone and there was nothing to reveal that they had ever been there save the faint clatter of loose stones following them down the slope.

The minutes passed leadenly. Pollacks began to count off the seconds under his breath, punctuated by the dying gasps of the man next to him. Then he heard the first harsh crunch of heavy seaboots on wet shingle. They had made the boat.

'Just one more minute, lads,' he whispered.

'Hope so, sir,' someone answered in the dark. 'Giving me the creeps up here, it is.'

Pollacks counted off the final sixty seconds. 'Okay,' he began as the moon slipped from behind the clouds again and flung its pitiless light on the handful of frozen exhausted men hidden below. Pollacks stopped short, fear constricting his throat. The moon's beams had already illuminated the long line of dark figures advancing slowly towards them, their rifles held at the port.

'Get out,' he forced himself to say. 'Get out – quick!'

As the moon disappeared again, the ratings broke cover, pelting down the slope towards the beach. A savage, ragged burst of gunfire tore apart the heavy silence. Pollacks staggered to his feet, blinded for an instant by the muzzle flashes.

'Run for it!' he bellowed and fired wildly at the advancing Norwegians.

'Don't leave me, sir, please,' whispered the dying rating.

'I'm not going to,' Pollacks assured him, as the Norwegians opened fire again, more accurately this time. 'Come on, we're getting out of here.' Bending down with a grunt as the slugs started to strike the snow all around him, he lifted him up.

Slowly they began to stagger after the rest. Behind them the Norwegians started to advance again. Down on the beach, Pollacks could hear the scrape of a boat's keel on the shingle. Now they were trying to push the longboat into the water. There was a cry of rage from their pursuers as they realised the British were getting away. The rating stiffened as the bullet slammed into his back with a soft thwack. He tore himself from Pollacks's grasp and fell dead in the snow.

Pollacks's relief was enormous. He had done his bit; he was free. Pistol in hand, he raced forward, his teeth bared like those of a wild animal. A dark shape barred his way, crying something in a language he did not understand. He fired automatically. The Norwegian screamed once then collapsed, clasping his hands to the burning fire of his stomach. Pollacks sprang over him.

Down below Degenhardt was bellowing, *'Come on, come on, we've nearly done it now!'*

His cry lent speed to Pollacks's feet. He flew down the slope, scattering rocks and stones on both sides. He glanced off a boulder and staggered to the right. A man loomed up. Hand trembling crazily, Pollacks fired and missed. The man sprang forward. A gleam of silver. The Norwegian was armed with the same sort of fish-gutting knife with which they had killed the policeman. Face contorted with fear, Pollacks pressed his trigger again. Nothing, but a harsh metallic click. His magazine was empty.

With a yell of triumph, the Norwegian was on him. Pollacks's face was swamped with his hot, foul breath as they thrashed and rolled on the snowy slope, Pollacks seeking desperately to ward off the flailing knife. A blinding pain shot through him, as his fingers clenched the razor-sharp blade. He brought up his knee and caught the Norwegian directly in the crotch. The Norwegian screamed and as the knife fell from his slack fingers, Pollacks grabbed it and slashed it savagely deep into his exposed throat.

Crazily, Pollacks staggered to his feet. Shambling like a drunken ape, his injured arm hanging slackly at his side, he continued his descent. Now he could make out the dark figures on the beach, backs bent, up to their knees in the white bubbling water, as they sought to launch the boat. In a minute, he'd reach them. Despite the burning pain of his hand, his scummed lips broke into a smile.

'I'm coming … coming,' he called hoarsely. 'Wait for me, lads, I'm com–'

The slug caught him squarely in the back of the thigh and threw him to the ground with a thud. A savage pain tore through his leg and made him sob. Yet he knew he could not succumb. As the sound of the running feet behind him drummed louder in his ears, he realised just how desperately he wanted to live.

'I'm coming,' he croaked as he began to crawl, his thigh a burning, throbbing agony, his stomach muscles tightening as he imagined a bayonet being thrust sickeningly into his back.

'All right, lads, get in!' Degenhardt shouted.

'But what about Jimmy Ballocks, Coxswain?' A coarse Liverpudlian voice protested. 'We can't leave him!'

'Don't you worry about Mister Pollacks, Scouse! He'll make it–' the rest of his words were drowned by the volley from the Norwegians.

Pollacks screamed as one of their bullets smashed into his shoulder and threw him down to the ground. Automatically he rolled to one side and the rest of the slugs hissed hotly into the snow. He tried to raise himself, but couldn't. The sound of the running feet was getting closer now. Whimpering and cursing in a frenzy of fumbling, he pulled out a handful of slugs from his pouch and fitted them into the pistol dangling by its white lanyard from his neck. The line of Norwegians was clearly outlined against the dark skyline.

Below, a frightened voice yelled, 'Come on, Coxswain, let's go, Jimmy Ballocks has had it! He'd have been here ages ago, if he hadn't! Coxswain Degenhardt, please!'

With a hand that had suddenly ceased trembling, he brought up the pistol as the splash of oars below indicated that they were going and the tall running shadow blotted out the night sky above him. He remembered MacFarland's protest. 'Jimmy Ballocks,' he grunted, 'so that's what they called me all along!'

He pressed the trigger. Above him, the Norwegian halted, his hands clawing at his chest and in the momentary scarlet stab of flame, he saw as he died that the man lying sprawled in the snow at his feet was smiling.

SIX

Doan hurtled the bowline over the stem of the sinking longboat. Behind him the rating at the engine prepared to reverse. Now the bullets were winging wickedly low over the surface of the water, and Doan could see the dark outlines of the enemy against the muzzle flashes.

'Secure her – for Chrissake, Degenhardt!' he yelled desperately and ducked as a bullet hissed through the night just above his head, *'Quick!'*

Spluttering with seawater and fury at the untidy mess on the beach, Degenhardt grabbed the wet line and fastened it to the bow. Next to him, half submerged, one of the wounded ratings groaned. At the stern, Scouse, firing wildly at the beach, cried, 'Duck!'

The dark egg of a grenade sailed above their heads and exploded only yards away. The sea heaved and the sinking longboat rocked crazily as it was swamped. Silver-gleaming slivers of metal hissed through the darkness.

'All secure, sir!' bellowed Degenhardt.

'Take her away!' Doan ordered above the

increasing volume of the Norwegians' fire.

The motorboat's engine took the strain. The water churned creamily. Between it and the holed longboat, the line tightened. They started to move away. Doan switched on the loud-hailer.

'All clear, Degenhardt?'

'Sir – Mr Pollacks didn't make it!'

Doan accepted the information unemotionally. He was wholly preoccupied with the task of saving the sinking longboat and its cargo of wounded, frightened men. He swung round and addressed the lean shape of the *Rose* some five hundred yards away, hoping that the loud-hailer would carry that far. 'Ahoy, the *Rose*... Here Doan, we're moving off now. Nobody left on the beach!'

Lamb reacted at once. As the two boats chugged away from the shore, the *Rose's* guns opened up. Later Doan swore that he had been able to see the five-inch shells as they sped from her guns towards the beach. An instant later the high explosive smashed into the surprised Norwegians. Six huge spurts of smoke, tinged with evil yellow flame, dug vast holes in the beach. For a fleeting second Doan caught a frightening glimpse of dark bodies being tossed like sacks through the air against the glowing background, then the light vanished, and as the echoing roar died away, the night was silent save for the sound of their own mightily labouring engine.

Lamb touched the tousled wet head of the green hand with the bloody gash in the side of his face, and straightened up to let the sick-bay attendant get on with his work of treating him and the other casualties.

'All right, lad,' he said softly to the youngster who was whimpering, 'we'll take care of you.'

He turned to Doan. 'Well?'

'One dead, six wounded, sir – and Mr Pollacks – er – missing.'

Lamb sighed. 'Poor old Pollacks,' he said softly and fell silent for a moment, knowing in his heart that it was better this way; better to die than face what would have been waiting for both of them once the *Rose* returned to England. He forced that miserable prospect out of his mind and asked, 'But who the hell were they – the people who attacked you?'

'Norwegians, sir,' Coxswain Degenhardt answered for Doan, nursing the wound in his arm with fingers through which the blood seeped darkly. 'Norwegian Fascists who support the Germans.' He winced with pain and in the dim green light, Lamb could see how pale his tough old battered face was.

'Thank you, Coxswain. Well, it doesn't matter much now, does it? Whoever they were, we've gone and lost the landing site.

The old *Rose* has gone and done it once again, it seems.' He shook his head. 'No matter. Coxswain, thank you for the information. Better let the sickbay tiffy have a look at that wound of yours next.'

'It's nothing sir. Just a scratch,' Degenhardt said almost aggressively. 'But there's something else, sir – something important.'

'What do you mean?'

Degenhardt swallowed hard. Behind him the medic was cutting the bloody cloth from a gaping, ragged wound in a rating's belly. 'Well, sir, we found a paper on one of them–' Swiftly he explained what he had read on the note taken from the dead radio operator.

'But that's impossible,' Doan objected. 'The *Braunschweig's* ten thousand tons. Hell, she wouldn't dare venture into a fjord like this!'

'Oh yes, she would,' Lamb interrupted, the calmness of his voice not reflecting the empty feeling he felt in his guts at that moment. 'At least in the main channel. For a ship of her size, she has a remarkably shallow draught. After all, she and her sister ships were partly built for operations in the Baltic narrows and the like–' he broke off suddenly. 'Thank you, Coxswain. Now go and get that wound treated.'

Reluctantly, the bedraggled Degenhardt slouched over to the sickbay attendants.

Lamb waited till he had gone and then

191

snapped to Doan: 'Come on, I've got something I want to discuss with you.'

In the wardroom Lamb waited until Doan had dumped his heavy pistol belt upon the table before he answered the unspoken question in the American's eyes: 'I think Degenhardt's reasoning is correct, Doan. You see I don't think the Jerries would have sent such a vital convoy all the way from their Baltic and North Sea ports to Narvik covered only by one single cruiser, the *Hipper*. What if they had run into the vanguard of the Home Fleet? How would the convoy's destroyers have coped with the battlecruisers, let's say the *Repulse* or the *Renown,* which they could have reasoned would be fast enough to get from Scapa to Norwegian waters in time, eh?' He looked at Doan almost accusingly. 'Their troopers would have been sitting ducks. Just like ours will be if Degenhardt is right and the *Braunschweig* is lurking out there somewhere waiting for them.'

Doan did not say anything, but his brow creased in a thoughtful frown.

'So for my money, Doan, that convoy would have been guarded by two cruisers. They would have been match enough for our World War One vintage cruisers. When *Hipper* turned back and the convoy had been safely run into Narvik, she set off to see what she could find in the way of easy pickings, just like the *Graf Spee* did in the

South Atlantic last year.'

For a moment he fell silent. Outside, the elderly wardroom steward was complaining in a whining tone to someone or other, 'But I tell yer, I cleaned the sods only yesterday. How can I help if they've gone green again! It must be the weather.'

'But if the *Braunschweig* is out there, skipper,' Doan asked slowly, 'what are *we* gonna do about it?'

'You know Captain Yorke's orders, don't you, Doan?'

The other man nodded a little miserably, 'Yeah, I know them well, skipper.'

'So you know I'm to hold my station here till I can signal the troopers' arrival. Besides you are well aware of his attitude to HMS *Rose* and, in particular, to its captain?' He laughed bitterly. 'Even if I dared break radio silence, how would I put it across to him? Do you think he would believe some cock-and-bull story of a bunch of Norwegian traitors signalling to a cruiser which is not supposed to be there in the first place. No, not Captain Vernon Yorke!'

'But skipper,' Doan objected, now obviously convinced that Degenhardt was right. 'What if the *Braunschweig* sailed into the main channel, managed to negotiate – say – the Tjeldsund, and holed up there before those troopers arrived. Then when their escorts had left, in the belief that our Flotilla would provide any muscle they might need, the *Braunschweig* opened fire.' He made the gesture of crooking a forefinger back and forth, as if he were pulling the trigger of a gun, '*sweet Jesus*, it'd be slaughter!'

'I know, Doan, you don't have to draw me a picture. They'd have no place to manoeuvre and the Jerry'd be able to pick them off one by one with those eight-inch guns of hers. By the time Captain Yorke arrived on the scene, they'd be at the bottom of the fjord feeding the fishes and the *Braunschweig* would be on her way out again at top speed.' He broke off, as if overwhelmed by the horrifying magnitude of the disaster that could threaten the troop ships, now only a matter of hours away from the fjord, and walked slowly over to the chart on the wall.

Thoughtfully he stared at the chart, tapping his front teeth with his forefinger. 'What do you think the range of the *Braunschweig's* guns is, Doan?'

Doan shrugged. 'Eight-inch guns – oh, my guess would be about twenty-seven thousand yards – broadside.'

'Yes, that would be about my guess. I should imagine the Jerries would try to get the max range out of them after London.'*

*The 1935 London Naval Treaty, limiting the number and type of ships to be built after that date by the great powers

194

He tapped his teeth again, sunk apparently in thought.

'That would give her the advantage of at least four thousand yards before we could even bring our five-inchers to bear.'

Doan's eyes gleamed. 'Yeah at that range our shells would bounce off her armour like ping-pong balls. After all, she's got at least five-and-a-half-inch-thick armour around her turrets.'

'I agree,' Lamb said. 'To be effective we'd have to be within three thousand yards – really effective, I mean.'

Doan attempted no longer to hide his hope. 'You don't mean, skipper, do you–'

Lamb laughed. 'I do. I don't know exactly how, but an idea is beginning to form up here,' he tapped his forehead.

'But what about Captain Yorke, skipper?' Doan objected.

Lamb grinned. 'By the time Captain Yorke finds out, he'll be writing up his recommendation for our gongs – or those nice little sad letters to our next-of-kins.'

FIVE: *THE BRAUNSCHWEIG*

'*Kameraden,* when we enter that fjord, we enter to do battle – holy battle – for our Führer. And we must win that battle, whatever the cost to ourselves. Some of you – perhaps many of you – will die. But of those who survive, the boys will return to Germany as men – and those of you who are already men, will be heroes!'

Kapitan zur See Hass to the crew of the Braunschweig, *April 10th, 1940*

ONE

'Volltreffer!'*

Kapitan zur See Hans Hass cried as the *Braunschweig's* first salvo struck the British minesweeper directly behind the bridge, sending fist-sized fragments of steel hissing over the little ship's deck, cutting down the surprised seamen almost before they knew what had hit them.

One of the auxiliary's fuel tanks burst almost at once as the ship heeled under the impact of the second salvo from the *Braunschweig's* eight-inch guns. Oil spilled out of it like red lava. In an instant the aft deck became a mass of flames. A fifty-foot-long blow torch roared down the companionways. Evil blue flames lapped greedily at the bubbling paintwork. The steel doors started to buckle outwards in the tremendous heat and as the screaming, smoke-blinded crew began to fling themselves overboard into the burning water, the upper deck burst into an inferno.

Kapitanleutnant Lutz, the *Braunschweig's* second-in-command, tore his eyes away

*Direct hit.

199

from the terrible sight and fixed his gaze on the Captain's face. Hollowed out to a lean death's head in the bloody light cast by the sinking ship, Captain Hass's features were animated by an animal expression of naked pleasure.

'*Herr Kapitan*,' Lutz said.

Hass did not seem to hear, his gazed fixed on the death throes of the minesweeper, and Lutz had to repeat his words once again before the Captain finally tore his eyes away from the terrible sight.

'Yes, Lutz?'

'We've broken her last message, sir. You were right. The minesweeper was clearing the way for the British invasion fleet. Four troopships protected by four destroyers and the battleships *Warspite* and the *Queen Elizabeth*.'

'*Grossartig!*' Kapitan zur See Hass slapped his knee delightedly in the manner affected, Lutz recalled from the newsreels, by the Führer himself, his prominent, pale blue eyes lighting up suddenly. 'So the Tommies are coming, as I thought! Good ... good.'

He swung round and for a moment focused his glasses on the harsh white mass of the Norwegian cliffs guarding the entrance to Westfjord. Somehow it reminded him of his first glimpse of the Alps as a youth: harsh, unyielding, challenging, the very symbol of the National Socialist creed to which he subscribed fervently, and which he knew would soon sweep away the effete Europe of the past and replace it by the New Order of the Führer's One Thousand Year Reich.

'We shall go in then, Lutz,' he decided, lowering his glasses abruptly, 'and wait for the Tommies behind that entrance. Once their escorts have left them, they'll be ours for the taking.' His eyes gleamed and he brought the fingers of his right hand together savagely, as if he were crushing some object to pulp. 'Not one of them will escape and we will show Herr Chamberlain with his umbrella that the German Navy is not made up of *Graf Spees.*'

Lutz's face remained cold. He did not share his commander's easy enthusiasms, which seemed the fashion these days among the younger National Socialist officers. As a cadet he had fought against the Tommies at Jutland and in 1918 he had sailed into Scapa with the surrendering Grand Fleet. He knew the British; they were not very aggressive, but they were tough and dogged in defence. They would not be the easy meat that people like Hass imagined.

'May I point out the difficulties – even dangers, Captain?' he said. 'The charts are not very accurate and with our draught–'

'*Mein lieber Lutz,*' Hass interrupted, barely concealing the contempt in his voice. 'Why must you always see difficulties where there are none? As our Führer Adolf Hitler,' he said the name as if it were in italics, 'has remarked often enough – "a National Socialist knows only the offensive. The defensive is the weakling's way out." Rest assured, I shall take all proper precautions. But whatever the danger, we must go into that fjord. Germany expects it of us.'

Lutz stifled a sigh just in time. How often had he heard those words in these last few years – 'Germany expects'? They were an excuse for many courses of action which it was better not to think too deeply about. 'I see, sir,' he answered. 'And the Tommies?' he indicated the survivors struggling frantically in the water, as the little mine-sweeper started to tilt over before sliding beneath the green, heaving waves for ever. 'Shall I order the ship to heave to to pick them up?'

Kapitan zur See Hass looked at his second-in-command as if he had suddenly gone out of his mind. 'Heave to, Lutz!' he exclaimed. *'Sie sind wohl nicht bei Trost, Mann!'* And risk being caught by Tommy aircraft! No, no, Lutz, that is simply outdated bourgeois sentimentality.'

'But the code of the sea, sir,' protested Lutz. 'We can't let them drown out there!'

*Are you quite right in the head?

'The new Germany cannot afford such luxuries as your so-called code of the sea. This new war must be fought on a life-or-death basis. I have no time for such German Christmas-tree sentimentality,' Hass sneered. 'Now then, let us not waste any more time on the matter. Get the seaplanes up. I want a thorough reconnaissance made of the fjord before we enter.' He threw a glance at his wrist watch. 'And assemble all hands in thirty minutes' time. I want to speak to them, remind them of their National Socialist duty and of the glorious opportunity that is now open to the *Braunschweig*. That is all, Lutz, you may go about your duties now.'

'Jawohl, Herr Kapitan!'

For a moment Hass stroked his jaw thoughtfully. 'Does Lutz think I do these things for effect?' he asked himself. 'Doesn't he realise that everything is a battle and that one has to be hard, not only on the enemy but also on oneself in order to win that battle?' Then he turned to the helmsman. *'Voller Fahrt voraus!'**

As the telegraph clanged and the great cruiser, the pride of the German Navy, surged ahead, he did not look back. The *Braunschweig's* mighty screws churned through the screaming Tommies, chopping

*Full ahead.

their helpless bodies to bloody lumps in the wild water.

In 1931, Hans Hass had served as the youngest member on the tribunal chaired by Admiral Raeder to enquire into the conduct of a tall, blond signals lieutenant with bold slanting eyes and the quick vital movements of a champion fencer. The officer was charged with unbecoming conduct, namely the seduction of a Kiel businessman's daughter. After promising to marry the girl, whose father was a personal friend of Raeder's, he had got her between the sheets and then conveniently forgotten his original promise because, as he had stated at his trial: 'As a German officer it went against my honour to marry a girl who was not pure.' Under Raeder's guidance, the Court had found the officer guilty and sentenced him to be cashiered from the Navy. Hass had been the only one to vote in the cashiered officer's favour, a decision which had gained him a cold, almost pitying smile from the sinister ex-Lieutenant. The name of the signals officer was Reinhard Tristan Heydrich.

Three years later, Heydrich had become Himmler's second-in-command, an SS General, and one of the most powerful men in the new Reich. Surprisingly enough, he had not forgotten the only man to vote for his acquittal at that trial and Hans Hass found himself moving up the ladder of promotion very quickly indeed. In 1937, when he had attended the British Coronation Naval Review, he was the second officer on the pocket battleship *Deutschland* and already a Lieutenant-Commander, promoted ahead of men years senior to him. By now he was a convinced National Socialist and when he was presented to the new British king, he had snapped his polished heels together and thrown up his right arm stiffly in the proud new 'German salute'. The British Press had been shocked. *'King Given Nazi Salute!'* screamed the headlines. Henderson, the British Ambassador in Berlin, had protested personally to von Ribbentrop, the Foreign Minister. Heydrich had called Hass to his office at Number 10 Prinz Albrechtstrasse in Berlin and told him that he was 'a damn fool'; his career was ruined. But Heydrich had been mistaken. Privately Hass had been informed by quarters close to the Führer that the 'Leader' admired his courage and that 'in the New Germany, National Socialist ships will be commanded solely by National Socialist captains'. One year later he had been given command of the *Braunschweig,* the newest ship in the Kreigsmarine; at the age of 37, the youngest full captain in the whole fleet.

From that proud moment onwards Hans Hass has known that Germany's destiny lay solely in the hands of the man his fellow officers called contemptuously behind his back 'that damned Bohemian corporal'. He had known too that the *Braunschweig* must represent not only the fleet, but the new 'One Thousand Year Reich', which the Führer was in process of creating. On the day that he had first put foot on the gleaming new cruiser which had the striking power of the average British battle-cruiser, he had sworn a holy oath to himself that he would dedicate the *Braunschweig* to the National Socialist cause.

On that afternoon, as he looked down at the assembled crew, with the sky already darkening to the west, he knew he must convince them that this, their battle, was of vital importance to the future of the New Germany.

'*Kameraden,*' he cried, listening to his voice echo and re-echo throughout the ship. 'In the old days, we older men thought first of our ship, then the Navy and finally of our Fatherland. Today that situation has changed.' Proudly he looked the length of his ship, all two hundred metres of her, lean, fast, compact, and dangerous. 'Today we owe our allegiance, *not* to our ship, our Navy, *not* to our Fatherland even, but to our Führer – *Adolf Hitler!*' He stiffened and looked down at their rigid, smart, blue-jacketed ranks, the long ribbons of their flat caps sailing in the wind. 'And what does that Führer expect from us? Unquestioning, absolute obedience and one hundred per cent dedication to the National Socialist cause. *Kameraden,* when we enter that fjord, we enter to do battle – holy battle – for our Führer. And we must win that battle, whatever the cost to ourselves. Some of you – perhaps many of you – will die. But of those who will survive, the boys will return to Germany as men – and those of you who are already men, will be herocs!'

As the first seaplane was catapulted high into the sky and sailed above the deck, blacking out the seamen's faces with its fleeting shadow, he clicked to attention and roared: *'Kameraden, sieg heil!'*

'Sieg heil!' the hoarse roar rose from their rigid, enthusiastic ranks, gathering momentum like a tidal wave racing up an estuary, until it swamped the thin-faced man standing to attention on the bridge, his eyes gleaming with the fire of the fanatic.

In the lee of the high cliffs, the surface of the water was broken by soft ice-mush which lay there like immense white mushrooms. Now there was no wind and it was only the occasional grey plume of smoke drifting from the stationary *Rose's* funnel in a lazy spiral upwards that indicated that the destroyer was still alive.

Carefully Scouse started to scatter ashes from the galley on the icy deck so that his crew would have some sort of foothold if the Captain called action stations during the night.

'Christ, Scouse,' said his oppo Bunts, who was off duty, 'you look like ruddy old Father Time himsen with that spade and bucket!' He flipped his Woodbine neatly over the side with his thumb and forefinger. 'Old Jerry's not gonna come now. Don't yer know that they bed down for the night at six in the German Navy?'

'Ay,' Scouse answered dourly, but not stopping his work, 'and if me Aunt Fanny had a moustache, she'd be me Uncle Joe! Don't try to cod me, Bunts, them Jerries is gonna turn up tonight. I can feel it in my bones.'

'You and yer bones,' Bunts scoffed. 'All you can feel in yer bones is that dose of siff you got in the Pit in '38 acting up–' Bunts stopped abruptly. 'What was that?'

'What was what?'

'That!'

Up on the bridge, a worried Lamb had heard the sound too and recognised it earlier than Bunts – the drone of a slow moving aircraft, searching for something. He leaned over the bridge and cupped his hands to his mouth. 'Ahoy, there, Mr Gowan.'

Gowan the Guns, muffled to the eyes in an ancient stained duffle-coat two sizes too big for him, popped his head round the edge of B-turret, his face barely visible in the faint white light. 'Sir?'

'Mr Gowan, no starshells, no ack-ack – nothing. If that plane's from the *Braunschweig,* I don't want her spotting our position. Understood?'

'Understood, sir!' Gowan dashed away to carry out his order, while the drone of the slow-flying plane grew steadily louder.

For three hours now, the *Rose* had been waiting, tucked in the lee of the four-hundred-foot-high cliffs that covered the entrance to the Westfjord, while Lamb had wrestled with his conscience, wondering whether he had done right by deserting his station. He would soon know whether he had been justified in doing so, for if the plane up there turned out to be a seaplane, it would be almost certainly one of the *Braunschweig's* reconnaissance seaplanes. Fingers gripping the edge of the bridge tensely, head cocked to one side in order to hear better, he waited for the plane to come closer. Beside him Doan trained his night glasses to the west, his breath coming in excited gasps.

Suddenly he began to fumble rapidly with

209

the adjustment. 'Got him, skipper!' he rapped.

'Well?' Lamb's hands gripped the bridge even harder.

'Sea ... yes, definitely a seaplane...'

'But is she a Jerry?'

Desperately the American worked the focusing wheel, as the roar grew louder. 'Yes,' he yelled, 'she is!... An *Arado*, yes, I'm certain. You can't mistake that wing...' He let the binoculars fall and stared at the skipper. 'You were right, sir. She must be from the *Braunschweig.*'

But Lamb had no time to compliment himself on the accuracy of his guess and the fact that the decision to leave his station against Captain Yorke's orders had been justified. As the plane started to cross over them, a dark shadow more sensed than seen in the still night sky, he prayed desperately that the *Arado* wouldn't spot the *Rose*.

It took the single-engined, slow seaplane a couple of seconds to pass over their hiding place in the lee of the cliff. They seemed an age to Lamb. But at last the plane's engine grew softer and with a sigh of relief Lamb knew she'd missed them.

'Phew,' he breathed out. 'We've done it–'

And in that instant the second *Arado* came in in a long glide from the land, its flare bursting into a dazzling whiteness that singed their eyeballs cruelly. Night became day. Rocking wildly from side to side under its little parachute, the flare floated above the ship, throwing her into startling relief, bathing the sea all around them in its brilliant glare.

'Knock out that flare!' shouted Lamb. 'Knock the bastard out – quick!'

Scouse reacted first. Dropping his bucket and scattering cinders everywhere, he pelted for A-turret. 'Get outa the sodding way,' he snarled and pushed the green hand at the sight to one side. In one and the same movement, he swung himself behind the sight and adjusted it, rapidly cranking the fire inchers upwards.

Now the seaplane was turning slowly to their west, a sinister black shadow on the fringe of the light.

Lamb held his breath, his face a taut death's head in the pitiless brilliance. If the pilot spotted them and reported their presence to the ship which had sent him on his mission, his whole plan would be doomed to failure.

The *Arado* came in low at one hundred miles an hour, seeming to skim the white-topped waves, still unaware of what was waiting for it in the circle of dying light. Lamb pressed the bridge rail. Why didn't A-turret open fire? But Scouse was biding his time. Tensely, hunched over the sight, he saw the seaplane grow larger and larger,

211

knowing that he would only get one chance. If he failed to hit the seaplane the first time, the *Arada* would break to port and that would be that.

'Come on, yer bugger,' he muttered urgently to himself. 'Come on and see what Daddy's got waiting!'

Suddenly the twin guns erupted, as if of their own accord. The twin H.E.* screamed through the night, trailing their white tails behind them. With a throaty crack, they exploded directly in the *Arado's* path. The white blob of the pilot's face disappeared behind a spider's web of broken perspex. The left wing snapped off and fluttered to the water like a falling leaf. Desperately but in vain, the pilot tried to control the crippled plane. Trailing a brilliant red flame behind it, the *Arado* roared down, a shattered, burning crucifix to smack into the hissing water only yards away from the destroyer now settling back into the cover of darkness.

'Great balls of fire, Scouse,' Bunts yelled, 'you got the bastard!'

From the deck came a ragged cheer. Lamb knew he had no time to waste on congratulations. 'Coxswain,' he cried, 'see if you can get that pilot on board. We've got to find out whether he radioed our position to

*High Explosive.

212

the *Braunschweig.*'

The Navy pilot lifted the cigarette Degenhardt had given him in his charred claw and placed it in the blackened hole, as if the Woodbine weighed a ton. Lamb fought back a desperate desire to vomit at the sight of his face, transformed by the fire into a bright pink, horrible skull.

He gasped: 'What did he say, Degenhardt – is he?'

Degenhardt tore his eyes from the mutilated pilot and nodded. 'Yessir. He's from the *Braunschweig,* sir.'

Opposite him, the dying pilot had begun to cough. Slowly, the Woodbine started to slip from his charred claw.

Lamb licked suddenly parched lips and forced himself to persist. 'Listen, Degenhardt, I want you to ask if he radioed our position back to his ship before he was shot down.'

'Ay, ay, sir,' Degenhardt snapped. 'I'll ask him, but–' he shrugged and left the rest of the sentence unfinished. 'Herr Leutnant,' he began.

Opposite him the pilot, slumped on the chair, opened his eyes wearily and stared at the Coxswain as if he were a creature from another world. '*Was?*' he croaked.

Degenhardt repeated his question, despair in his voice.

Again the dying man looked at him, blank-eyed. *'Ich sterbe,* * he sighed.

'What did he say, Coxswain?' Lamb asked.

Degenhardt translated. Lamb's face hardened bitterly. He could see the German was dying fast. But he could not be allowed to escape to the blessing of death without having answered the all-important question. 'Coxswain, force him, force him to answer!' he demanded.

'Hoeren Sie zu, Herr Leutnant, ** Degenhardt tried again. *'Herr Leutnant, Herr Leutnant, bitte.'*

But the pilot did not open his eyes.

'Degenhardt, we must have that inform-ation!' Lamb rapped, his voice harsh and unyielding.

The Coxswain gulped. The pilot could not have been more than nineteen. 'A green beak,' they would have called him once in the old Navy, 'still wet behind the spoons'. And now he was dying in enemy hands, hardly even aware where he was, concerned solely with the pain which racked his cruelly burned body.

'Herr Leutnant – please,' he cried. 'You must answer!'

'Hit him!' Lamb barked. 'Hit him, if he won't answer. Do you hear!'

*I'm dying.
**Listen, Lieutenant.

214

Petty Officer Degenhardt raised his hand, the hand which had killed the SA man so long before. Now he knew as he brought it down across the boy's terrible pink face that it was going to kill anther fellow countryman.

The boy whimpered. But his eyes did not open. The scarlet blood was pouring from his black lips. Death could only be a matter of moments away now.

'Hit him again!' Lamb ordered through gritted teeth.

'Skipper, for God's sake!'

Lamb did not hear Doan's muffled protest. His whole attention was on the dying man, as Degenhardt raised his hard hand once again and brought it down across the pilot's face.

The pilot groaned and his eyes flickered open. Degenhardt leaned forward hastily, overcoming his nausea by a sheer effort of will, bringing his tough old face close to that of the pilot's. 'Listen, Lieutenant, did you radio our position or the fact you had sighted us back to the *Braunschweig?* Did you?'

'*Nein,*' he whispered, the blood bubbling on his lips as he spoke. '*Ich hatte keine Zeit, weil–*' His head dropped to his chest. He was dead.

Lamb gulped. 'Well?' he demanded, trying desperately to keep his voice under control.

'What did he say?'

Slowly Degenhardt raised himself from the dead boy, the tears streaming down his leathery old cheeks. 'No, sir ... he didn't have time.'

TWO

Dawn came late. For a few moments the pale Arctic sun peered over the heaving horizon and lay there on the lip of sea, too feeble, it seemed, to rise any further. Then the snow began again and obscured it altogether. Steadily, like a grey ghost, the *Braunschweig* slid through the whirling white mass towards the entrance of Westfjord.

On the bridge Kapitan Zur See Hass stared along the sleek, menacing length of the ship. Every man and everything was in its correct place. His ship was a perfect German fighting machine, science and savagery welded into one to destroy the Führer's enemies. Satisfied with what he saw, the Captain turned to his second-in-command.

'Well, Lutz? What news of the *Arado?*'

Lutz shook his head slowly. 'Nothing, Captain. I'm afraid that young Dietz has had it. Poor kid, he was only nineteen – straight from Muerwik.'*

Hass gave an impatient sigh. 'His parents will be proud of him. He has died a hero's death for Folk, Fatherland and Führer! You

*German Navy training school.

217

will write to them that he died preparing the way for our heroic mission. Now what did the other pilot report?'

'The estuary is clear, sir. Further up, in the vicinity of Narvik, he spotted several Tommy destroyers.'

Hass did a quick calculation. 'Sixty kilo-metres roughly,' he muttered to himself. 'Speed thirty knots on average... Hm,' he raised his voice. 'It would take them perhaps a couple of hours to steam to the Westfjord by the time they had been alarmed. We could be back in the open sea by that time.' He laughed throatily. 'Perhaps we could tempt the Tommies to follow us. Then with the space to manoeuvre the sea offers us, we could well give them a taste of Krupp steel, eh, Lutz?'

The second-in-command forced himself to smile, but inwardly he told himself the Captain was taking far too many risks. Once inside the narrow confines of the Westfjord, the *Braunschweig* might find it impossible to use its tremendous 8-inch guns. Then there were the mines, and once a destroyer, with its greater manoeuvrability and shallower draught, got within torpedo range the cruiser could find itself in trouble.

'I don't like this business with Dietz, sir,' he ventured. 'One of the lookouts thought he heard gunfire just after Dietz sent his last location signal.' He frowned. 'Perhaps he did run into the Tommies up there.'

'Oh, you know those young sailors,' Hass returned. 'They're still unblooded. They're seeing ghosts. Once this day is done that will all change, believe me, Lutz.'

'You are determined to go in, sir?'

'*Selbstverständlich*, Lutz,' Hass snapped. 'What else? The fat, soft Tommies are ours for the taking. By this time tonight their troopships will be at the bottom of the estuary over there and I do not doubt for one moment that there will be those of us who will find that their throatache has been cured very suddenly.' He chuckled and nudged his second-in-command in the ribs, one hand fingering his neck, where hopefully the Knight's Cross or the Iron Cross would soon be dangling.

'Yessir,' Lutz answered mechanically. 'And your orders, Captain?'

'Orders,' Hass echoed. 'This is the *Braunschweig's* holy baptism of fire. There can be only one order – attack and destroy!'

The cold was intense. Those keeping watch on the *Rose's* gleaming deck, exposed to the bitter wind whistling in from the polar ice-cap, felt the deadly chill creep slowly upwards from feet to thighs, from thighs to shoulders, reaching out icily from the face, and then prayed to be relieved, even though they knew that they would be tortured by

219

the excruciating agony of returning circulation as soon as they returned to the warmth.

On the bridge Lieutenant Doan stamped his leaden feet and cursed at regular intervals under his breath. His whole body was chilled to the bone; his very heart seemed to have stopped beating. Now he stood, crouched like an old man, head ducked into the hood of his duffle-coat, hands dug deep into its pockets, cursing the cold, cursing the wind, cursing the war and, above all, cursing the *Braunschweig* for taking so damn long to appear.

Beside him Commander Lamb did not seem to notice the biting cold, swept in by a wind increasing in strength every second, and shrieking through the frozen rigging like a virago. Tirelessly he swept his binoculars back and forth ahead of them, searching the horizon for the first sign of the ship they had planned to destroy, his face purple with the cold, but with not a sign of fatigue.

'God, how the hell does he do it?' Doan asked himself under his breath and knew the answer to the question almost before he had posed it. The Captain was a professional who had trained all his life for moments like this: a professional who could forget the fact that he was taking a calculated risk by abandoning his position, that if he failed now, he wouldn't stand a cat's chance in hell at his court-martial. 'Yeah,' a cynical little voice at the back of his head quipped, 'if he lives, if any of us live that long!'

'Doan,' the Captain's voice cut into his frozen reverie urgently. 'Over there – to port! Do you see what I see?'

Doan swung up his binoculars, focused them in a frenzy of fumbling, and strained his eyes trying to penetrate the white gloom.

'Beyond the point,' the Captain cried excitedly. 'I just got it and then the snow–'

'Hot shit!' Doan breathed, half in awe, half in fear, as the menacing shape slid into the round circle of glass, 'it's her – it's the *Braunschweig,* skipper!'

'Yes, the *Braunschweig,*' Lamb echoed in relief. 'She turned up after all.' He pushed back his battered old cap and wiped his brow almost as if he were sweating. 'All right, Mr Doan, keep your fingers crossed and pray that the old *Rose* won't let us down this time. Sound action stations!'

As the loudspeaker finally clicked off, the crew tensed at their stations. And in A-turret Scouse fixed his cold eyes on the ship sailing unawares into the skipper's trap and began singing tonelessly under his breath:

'Up came a spider and sat down beside her,

221

Whipped his old bazooka out and this is what he said: "Get a hold o' this, bash-bash. Get hold o' that, bash-bash"…'

Kapitan zur See Hass wiped the lenses of his Zeiss glasses clean and took another look at the dark, white-flecked water which tumbled back and forth at the entrance to Westfjord. All around stood his officers and petty-officers, feet straddled against the roll of the ship as she met the water rushing out from the estuary. The men, he told himself, were functioning at top-pitch. In spite of their lack of combat experience, they were as good as any he had known in his nineteen years of service. When the time came they would give a good account of themselves.

Hass lowered his glasses and rubbed his eyes. They felt as if someone had thrown a handful of sand at them, they were so raw and heavy. But he knew he could not relax for an instant. With such a large ship in the confines of the narrow channel they were now entering, he could not drop his guard for a single second.

'*Achtung, Brücke*,' the young voice abruptly cut into his thoughts, '*Minen!*'

Ten pairs of binoculars swept round to port. Some twenty metres away a dark horned globe had suddenly appeared, bobbing up and down on the swaying surface of the water.

'Dead slow,' barked Hass, pulling at the telegraphs. 'Lutz,' he ordered, as the long cruiser started to slow down. 'Men with rifles on the port bow–' But his words were interrupted by an urgent cry from starboard.

'Mines, sir. Starboard!'

Lutz licked suddenly dry lips. A similar bobbing ball of deadly metal was floating on the other side of the *Braunschweig,* barring the main channel. 'Captain,' he began, but Hass cut him short.

'Don't panic, Lutz. Your average minefield is highly overrated. Obviously the Norwegians have laid it to block the main channel. If we cut across its corner towards the shallows we should be as safe as if we were sailing a dinghy up Laboe Fjord at Kiel.' He raised his voice. 'All right, stand by with rifles and boat-hooks… Hard to port, dead slow ahead.'

'But sir,' Lutz objected. 'The shallows sir! If we get caught on them…' His voice died away. Kapitan zur See Hans Hass was not even listening.

'Wow,' breathed Doan, as he and the Captain followed the *Braunschweig's* change of course, 'the Heinies have bought it! Old Chippy's trash cans fooled them.'

Lamb grinned. Chippy's cut down galley ashtins, with bits of hurriedly shaped wood to represent the horns of a mine stuck on them, had apparently tricked the Jerries. They were now leaving the main channel and moving close to the cliffs where the *Rose* was hidden, leaving themselves with virtually no room to manoeuvre. But there was no time to gloat over their little trick. Despite the shocking visibility, it would only be a matter of moments now before the *Braunschweig's* look-outs spotted the little destroyer, rocking back and forth on the swell under the shelter of the towering white cliffs. Everything depended upon Gowan the Guns and his torpedo tubes. If he missed with his deadly two-ton 'fish', that would be the end of HMS *Rose*.

The sub-lieutenant crouched over the torpedo-switch panel, his eyes tense as he waited for his men to report. Then it came through. 'Torpedoes closed up, sir!'

Gowan licked his lips and whispered a quick prayer in Welsh. 'Stand by torpedo attack,' he called into the phone.

'Ay, ay, sir.'

The sub bent his head over the three-pronged sight, his hand on the torpedo-firing button, his shiny blue bottom sticking up in the air. As the *Braunschweig* slid into his sights, he stabbed the firing buttons hard with this thumb. Once, twice, three times.

The *Rose* shuddered violently. From aft there came three rapid hushes of com-

224

pressed air. One after another, the two-ton fish slid into the water and their props began to rotate. For a second, the water was churned up wildly. Then they were under the sea's surface running at forty-fifty knots, bearing a white trail behind them, as they shot towards their target.

Up on the bridge, Doan and Commander Lamb swung their glasses round as one and focused their lenses on the faint white bubbling trails. Under his breath, Doan started to mutter fervently, 'Don't let them see the bastards ... don't let them see 'em!'

And crouched low in A-turret, Scouse's ribald monotonous account of the goings-on of 'Miss Muffet and the Spider who sat down beside her' came to an abrupt halt, the words frozen on suddenly taut lips.

'Torpedo – port bow!' screamed the look-out hysterically.

'Starboard ten!' Hass barked. 'Quick!'

The *Braunschweig* answered at once. As the white wake of the first torpedo hissed by in a straight, arrow-headed line, the lean cruiser heeled to starboard, sending instruments clattering to the deck in the charthouse.

'Torpedo – starboard, sir!' the panic-stricken cry came from the deck below.

The *Braunschweig's* slender bow knifed round. In a flurry of white water the second torpedo missed her by mere metres. Next to the Captain, Lutz gave a sign of relief. Hass had done it again. He took his handkerchief out of his pocket and was just about to mop his suddenly damp brow when the two look-outs screamed as one, '*Torpedo – midships!*'

The handkerchief fluttered from Lutz's hand. He tensed, waiting for the murderous blow. This time Hass could not manoeuvre the ship out of danger. An instant later he heard the hollow boom of metal striking metal. Lutz's nerve snapped. Fear swept over him in an uncontrollable flood. He could hear himself shouting incoherently that this was the end.

But the *Braunschweig* sailed on majestically, ever closer to the sudden enemy in the lee of the high white cliffs to port. The torpedo had failed to explode.

Commander Lamb crashed his fist down hard on the bridge rail. 'Two misses – and the third failed to explode!'

Doan looked at him, grey-faced and cowed. Glumly he nodded. 'Yeah, the sonuvabitch has let us down again, skipper!'

Lamb pulled himself together and turned to look where a mile away the *Braunschweig* was swinging round gracefully, her knife-like bows slewing towards their hiding place under the cliffs. 'She's going to attack!'

'Home!' shouted the number one.

Number two rammed in the charge and sprang back to allow the third man to lock the great breech.

'Ready!'

Up at the slit under the roof of the turret, Leutnant Goetz brought down his hand stiffly. Obermaat Krause pressed the trigger of the director. Detonators smashed into the cordite charges. The cordite exploded like a mad clap of thunder. The pressure shot the 200-pound shells up the twenty-five foot long barrels. At four times the speed of sound, they left the 8-inchers' muzzles. With the impact of a railway locomotive striking the muzzles at fifty kilometres an hour, the blast struck home. But by the time the blast encountered the turret's recoil system that tremendous shock had been completely absorbed and the two guns moved backwards as gently as an elderly granny leaning back in her cushions.

The *Rose* staggered under that awesome impact. The great shells struck the destroyer with the force of an express train travelling at sixty miles an hour, hurtling ashen-faced men to all sides. The first one hit B-turret. Its steel armour split open under the impact, glowing white-hot as it did so. A hissing fragment cleaved Gowan's neck in half so that his dark head, suddenly coloured crimson, toppled on to his chest like the head of a broken doll. Next to him a rating died as the searing blast burst his lungs, his eyes full of dying horror at the red cascade of the officer's blood pouring on to his outstretched hands.

The second hit the *Rose* amidships, penetrating right to the wardroom. The heat of its explosion was that of an oxy-acetylene burner. The wardroom's paint, the padding in the scuffed old chairs, the faded lino on the floor all burst into flame. The bottle of pink gin in the elderly steward's hand exploded, scattering fire over his panic-stricken face.

Sick and shaken, the blood pouring from a cut in his forehead, Lamb staggered to his feet on the bridge. He gazed at the confused mangled ruin of B-turret, his eyes wide and staring, as if unable to understand what had happened. Then he was in charge again, yelling order after urgent order, as the brazen lights on the *Braunschweig* indicated another murderous salvo.

'She's making smoke!' Hass cried exuberantly. 'She's going to try to make a run for it. But by God, she won't get away with it!' He turned to the helmsman, his face bright with triumph, 'Take her closer, helmsman. We're going to finish her off.'

'Captain,' Lutz protested desperately, 'the s–' His protest was drowned by the chatter of the port Oerlikons, followed a second later by a stream of bright red tracer curving towards the stricken British destroyer. 'Captain,' he yelled, cupping his hands around his mouth to make himself heard above the noise, 'the shoals!'

'We've got plenty of draught still,' Hass cried, his eyes blazing with the thrill of the chase. 'We're not going to let that impertinent little Tommy get away now. Helmsman, half speed ahead... Careful as you go now!'

'*Captain!*' Lutz yelled above the sharp vicious crackle of the 20mm shells stitching a white frenzied pattern across the intervening water. '*Captain!*'

But Kapitan zur See Hand Hass was not listening. His lean face was set in the wolfish expression of primitive man going in for the kill.

And as Lutz watched he heard a shattering crash, followed an instant later by a heartbreaking rending sound. The *Braunschweig* heeled to one side, throwing up a column of white water at her stern. For what seemed a long time it appeared to hang there. Then it crashed down, drenching the men hanging on grimly for their lives, as the pride of the German Navy ran aground.

THREE

Lamb, a dirty towel held to his bleeding head-wound, started his inspection of the stricken ship as soon as she had limped into the cover of the fjord leading up to Tjeldsund.

Most of the superstructure had gone. In its place there was a mound of grotesquely twisted metal. In B-turret, everyone was dead. Apart from Gowan, the gunners were poised at their stations, apparently unharmed and unmarked save for the tiny blobs of congealed black blood at the side of their open mouths which told Lamb of death by blast.

Below, everything was chaos. In the mess decks the sailors' metal lockers had broken adrift, vomiting forth their contents so that now letters and books and photographs were mixed with smashed pots and bottles of rum in insane confusion, while the shocked sailors knelt and tried to sort the mess out.

Finally Lamb knew the extent of the damage and went back to the bridge. He leaned gratefully against the canvas screen, now holed by flying shrapnel, and dabbed the bloody towel against his head. It was beginning to snow again, the flakes settling sadly down on the jumbled, battle-littered deck as if they did not wish to disturb the stricken ship's grief. But Lamb did not notice the snow. His mind was still full of the crew's faces as he had toured the ship. In spite of what the *Rose* had suffered in those terrible five minutes at the entrance to Westfjord, the men's faces expressed a kind of numbed, desperate resolve. At last, after weeks of trying, his 'baa-lambs', as he knew his men were called derisively by the crews of other ships, were a unified, determined crew. If the *Rose* had failed him, his men had not. Old hands, green hands, spivs – all of them were resolved to fight to the end.

'Skipper,' a voice said softly. It was Doan, his helmet gone somewhere or other during the brief fight, his hair covered in melting snowflakes.

'Yes?'

'The casualties, sir,' Doan said, lowering his eyes suddenly.

'Bad?'

Doan nodded. 'Gowan is dead, as you know. Ferris too. So that leaves you and me–'

'And the men?' Lamb interrupted him.

'Sixteen in all, if you exclude the lightly wounded.'

Lamb nodded his thanks slowly. 'Thank you, Mr Doan. What's the situation in the engine room? How are they getting on down there?'

'The ER9 estimates that he can get the engines back to full power within the next two hours.'

Lamb breathed out hard. 'Sparks just picked up a message from the troopship convoy. They're only two hours sailing time from Westfjord. According to their estimate, the troopers expect to enter just before dusk.'

'But can't we warn them what's waiting for them?'

'No,' Lamb shook his head glumly. 'Sparks can receive, but he can't send. It's something technical. Beyond me...'

'But skipper,' Doan cried, 'those poor dogfaces will be slaughtered if they don't have the cover of the escorts! Jesus, we must do something!'

Down below they were beginning to spread out the dead on the littered deck, each still shape shrouded in a blue naval blanket. The scene was as sombre as Lamb's mood.

'I know. I want you to get on to that engineer down there. Promise him a barrel of best whisky, if you like, but I want him to have those damned engines of his back at full power within the next hour. I'm going to need all the muscle I can get.'

Doan's tired face lit up. 'You mean we're

going in again, skipper?'

'Right in one, Doan. We must stop those troopers from being massacred – and the only way to do that is to attack the *Braunschweig*. As soon as the engines are back in shape, Doan, we're going in again!'

Kapitan zur See Hass had recovered almost at once from the shock of the *Braunschweig's* grounding. He rapped out a series of confident orders in a manner that had even Lutz's eyes glowing with undisguised admiration.

'Double watch on both bows ... increased air guard ... *Arado* up on immediate air patrol ... volunteers to scale the cliffs to prevent a surprise land attack ... torpedo nets out...'

Within the hour, he had the trapped ship as securely under control and protected from air, land, and sea attack as could be expected under the circumstances. Now he was puffing at one of his favourite 10 pfennig cigars, confident that he was completely in charge of the new situation.

'As I see it, Lutz,' he lectured, punctuating his remarks with hard puffs, 'with a bit of luck, we'll be off by four. High tide is expected then and the difference between our draught and the present depth is only a matter of a couple of metres.' He chuckled throatily. 'As we come off this damned

233

shoal, the Tommy troopships should be coming in through the strait over there – right into our guns.

'Naturally that Tommy who escaped will have radioed his comrades further up the fjord that we are here, but as I said before they will not make it in time. The only danger could be if they have aircraft with them, and as far as I know the Tribals don't carry planes. Anyway that cliff up there to port is as good as a bunker wall. They'd have a devil of a time getting in at us at low level with that thing barring their way.'

'But the troopships' escorts,' Lutz protested softly, wishing for reasons he couldn't quite explain to deflate the bubble of the Captain's enormous self-confidence. 'What about them?'

Hass shrugged easily. 'Let them come, Lutz. They would have to enter one by one to tackle us. And I am confident that Krupp steel can take all that the Tommies can throw at it – and throw plenty more back to boot. We'd be the undoubted victor if they tried that.' He puffed happily at his cheap cigar. *'Nein, mein lieber Lutz, sobald wir hier freikommen, kann nichts schief gehen, glauben Sie mir.'**

---

*'No, my dear Lutz, as soon as we're free, nothing can go wrong, believe me.'

FOUR

The engines were repaired. In the crew's quarters the old hands, faces set and drawn, were changing into their fresh underwear and number ones. If they were hit, they knew they would stand less chance of getting infected by gas gangrene if the cloth driven into their wounds were clean. The green hands watched the ritual in silence, preferring, it seemed, to die dirty. One or two of them went off to the heads to pray, away from the prying gaze of the others.

In his tiny cabin, the Coxswain thrust his shaving mirror down the front of his trousers and cursed when he saw how it bulged. *'Birnenarsch und Pflaumenkompott!'** he swore, using German, as he always did when he was alone, and wrenched it into place. Still it bulged awkwardly. But at least nobody was going to shoot him in the eggs.

In A-Turret, Scouse checked his ready ammunition carefully, whistling *Jealousy* through his gritted teeth, thinking of Liverpool and the Judies waiting in the pubs off the Gladstone Dock, ready to open them

*'Pear arse and stewed plums!'

235

pearly gates for a port n' lemon and one of each twice – with salt and vinegar, but not missing a thing, although his mind was a thousand miles away from that bleak green Norwegian seascape.

And down below Doan and Lieutenant Commander Lamb watched as the elderly ER9 carried out his last test before they could sail. Levelling up the bottle of silver nitrate in his greasy hand, he shook a couple of drops of the solution into the test-tube of boiler water he held in his other hand. Very carefully he shook the test tube and squinted along its length. Nothing. He shook the test tube once again.

Behind him Lamb smiled faintly. Next to him Doan shook his head disbelievingly. Before they could go to their deaths, the ER9 had to satisfy himself that no seawater was leaking from the condenser into the rest of the engine system. If there was, its salt would eat through the joints and tubes and cripple the *Rose* within a couple of hours.

Satisfied, the ER9 flung the contents of the test-tube on the deck. 'No salt,' he announced gravely. 'I mind, we're ready to sail, Captain.'

Lamb beamed. 'I mind too, Chief.'

'Christ,' Doan breathed for his part and earned himself a hard look from the ER9, who disapproved of blasphemy, 'what a way to fight a war!'

Back on the damaged bridge Lamb took a last look at the shattered superstructure, his face grey and haggard under the monk's hood of his dripping duffle-coat, then he gave the orders for the ship to get under way.

At precisely 15.00 hours, HMS *Rose* slipped her moorings and began to steam slowly down the narrow fjord. In the grey half-light under the leaden lowering clouds of an approaching Arctic dusk, she slid through the still water like an unsubstantial ghost. But despite her mangled turret, the gaping black hole amidships and her aft boats hanging from the davits at a crazy angle, she still had her guns and her engines. She was returning to wreak her revenge on those who had so badly damaged her. Grey, ghost-like and grim she disappeared into the gloom.

Finally Hass tore his gaze from the dark smudges staining the horizon. 'It's them all right, Lutz,' he said softly. 'The Tommy troopers.'

Lutz at his side on the bridge, muffled in his ankle-length leather coat, lowered his glasses. 'Yes, you're right, Captain.'

'*Punktlich wie die Mauerer!*'*

'Yes, right on time, sir.'

*As punctual as the bricklayers.

'What's the situation with the tide, Lutz? What is the latest estimate?'

'Another hour, I'm afraid, sir. There's still a difference of about two metres fifty.'

'Impossible – another hour!' Hass said fiercely. 'I cannot wait that long! What if that convoy spots us before we get off? They could still turn about you know. For the moment they are entering our little spiders' web like tame flies. But once they are alarmed, those flies can fly away – and what in three devils' name could we do, if we're stuck on this shoal? Great crap on the Christmas tree, Lutz, we must get off sooner than that! We must lighten the ship – radically. All unnecessary personal gear is to go overboard.'

'The men won't like it sir.'

'Unimportant. Lutz! What do a few paltry trinkets matter when we are fighting for Germany's future?'

While the lines of the sweating, cursing sailors doubled back and forth across the wet deck, dumping their pathetic bits and pieces over the side, and the troopers grew ever larger on the grey horizon, Kapitan zur See Hass hung over the gleaming brass railing at the *Braunschweig's* bow and watched the level of the water anxiously. She was coming off, he could see that, but not quick enough. Another half hour and the Tommies would be within range. But it would be almost dark by then and if they spotted the *Braunschweig,* they might well be able to escape into the gloom. He straightened up, his face dripping with spray from below, his hard face set in a worried frown.

'Lutz,' he barked, 'Commander Lutz!'

Lutz ran across the deck, his leather coat flapping around his ankles. 'Sir?' he panted breathlessly.

'This is no good,' Hass complained. 'We're not moving off quickly enough. My God, if the Tommies catch us without our trousers now, they might well give us a nasty kick up the arse! We must lighten her more. We must have several tons of Old Man* down below. We'll have to survive the rest of this cruise on bread and sausage. We Germans must learn to be hard. Overboard with it. See if that does the trick.'

But it did not. Despite the lessening of her weight, the *Braunschweig* stubbornly refused to budge from the sandbank. Through his glasses, Hass was beginning to be able to make out the details of the troopers' superstructure. Time was running out. He bit his bottom lip in anger.

In the end he called Lutz to him. 'Lutz, we

*Standard German military ration, called 'Old Man' because it was reputedly made of dead old men.

239

must get rid of the torpedo netting. The stuff is a terrible weight. I am confident that by ridding ourselves of that, we'll pull it off.'

Lutz looked at the Captain's lean face, aghast. 'But sir, that's tempting fate, isn't it? We're not off yet and are unable to manoeuvre. If we drop the torpedo netting and anyone manages to break through, well–'

'No one will manage to break through, Lutz!' Hass interrupted. 'And even if some damn Tommy did, he wouldn't have a chance in hell against us. Now, Lutz, get on with it. I want that torpedo netting overboard in the next fifteen minutes.'

'Now this is the plan, Doan,' Lamb said as the *Rose* drew nearer the entrance to Westfjord. 'We leave here at thirty knots, hoping we'll take the *Braunschweig* by surprise before she can let us have a broadside. By the time the *Braunschweig* has spotted us and starts to guess our course, I'm hoping, thanks to Chippy, that her captain will assume we daren't head for the minefield he thinks is out there. I imagine that he will be expecting us to swing round and head straight for him. At least I hope so, because if he isn't, one accurate salvo from those eight-inchers of his and the *Rose* has bought it.'

'You can say that again, skipper.'

THE LAST ATTACK ON THE *BRAUNSCHWEIG*

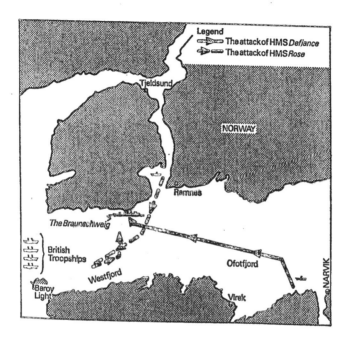

'So, if we're allowed – say – five minutes without any reaction from the *Braunschweig,* we're heading for the centre channel, making as much smoke as the cylinders can produce. My estimate is that within three minutes those five smoke cylinders of ours will have produced a smoke bank nearly a mile long – too long for the *Braunschweig* to be able to watch the whole length of it and react as soon as we come through it again – to the attack!'

Opposite him, Doan did a quick calculation. Allowing for normal spread, the smoke bank would be about a quarter of a mile thick. But at the speed the *Rose* could pass through it diagonally, it would probably take her about a minute to cross it. 'So all in all, the whole business, laying the smoke screen and crossing it to the attack, would take about five minutes, skipper?'

'Right, Doan. In essence, we'll have about ten minutes once we've left this fjord. You see I want to lay the screen so that its centre is not more than three thousand yards away from the *Braunschweig.*' His face hardened again. 'This time, those damned torpedoes had better not miss.'

'She's coming off, Lutz!' Kapitan zur See Hass cried in delight. 'What did I tell you? I knew it would work once we'd rid ourselves of the nets.'

242

The *Braunschweig* gave a huge shudder. There was an unpleasant rending sound from below her keel, as the water struck her again. Her plates vibrated with the impact.

'Lutz,' Hass ordered, straightening up from where he bent over the railing. 'Get everyone on the deck over to starboard – immediately. That should do it.'

The order echoed metallically from the speakers. The *Braunschweig* gave a mighty creak. Again she shuddered.

'Everyone on the starboard to commence jumping now!' Hass snapped.

In other circumstances, Lutz would have found the sight of scores of officers and men jumping up and down like a pack of crazy schoolchildren in the middle of some God-forsaken Norwegian fjord ludicrous, but not now, for he knew just how vital it was to get the stranded cruiser free before the enemy appeared. Without those torpedo nets she was helpless.

'One more time!' Hass bellowed excitedly, as the *Braunschweig* creaked and groaned like a gigantic metal mother giving birth.

The alarmed, almost hysterical cry of the port look-out blotted out his next words. *'Smoke to port, sir ... enemy destroyer bearing west...'*

The *Rose* was flying through the water of Westfjord, hitting each wave as if it were solid, her forecastle awash with angry white water. From her rakishly tilted funnel smoke began to pour, at first in thin wisps and then in a thick, greasy cloud that had the ratings to windward coughing and retching.

On the bridge Lamb felt his heart rise into his throat as if it were about to choke him, and he was forced to swallow to relieve the extreme nervous tension. It was now or never. If the *Braunschweig's* captain out-guessed him at this range and opened fire, the *Rose* would be blown to kingdom come. Then the smoke submerged him and he was coughing joyfully, the tears streaming down a face beaming with relief.

Two minutes passed without any reaction from the *Braunschweig*, now completely hidden from view by the thick bank of smoke. Lamb swung round and stared behind him. The grey smoke, tinged with oil, trailed behind him as far as he could see. He turned to Degenhardt, who had taken over the helm from Doan.

'Coxswain, I'm turning to port in a second. Stand by.'

'Ay ay, sir.'

Lamb picked up the tube. 'Doan – bridge.'

'Ay ay, sir.'

'I'm turning to port, now Doan. It'll take us a couple of minutes to double back and perhaps one more to break through the screen. You should find the *Braunschweig* at about red five when we're in the clear again. Shoot when you're ready and this time don't let those fish miss!'

He refitted the cap and leaning over the bridge, shouted to Scouse, 'Stand by A-turret. Three minutes and we'll be through.'

'Ay ay, sir!' the coarse Liverpudlian voice yelled back.

Lamb licked his lips and took a last look around him. Every man was at his station. 'Stop making smoke,' he ordered. 'All right, Coxswain, port fifteen!'

Degenhardt swung the wheel. The *Rose* heeled as she swung round. At full speed she raced back the way she had come. Suddenly their nostrils were full of the nauseating stink of fuel oil.

'All right,' Lamb gasped, trying to beat the smoke away from his eyes. 'In we go.'

Degenhardt swung the wheel again. Now they were beginning to cross the smoke bank. Lamb peered at his wrist-watch, his heart beating like a trip-hammer with excitement. 'Two minutes now, Doan,' he called over the tube.

A hush fell over the *Rose* now as the ship was engulfed by the gloomy darkness of the smoke muffling the sound of the waves and the wind.

'One minute, Doan,' Lamb said, his voice sounding very far away. They were nearly through. Lamb looked at the green glowing dial of his wrist-watch. 'Thirty seconds, Doan,' he called hoarsely.

'Ay ay, skipper.'

Lamb gripped the bridge-rail. Next to him, Degenhardt spread his legs and opened his mouth automatically, knowing that the blast might well puncture his ear-drums. The smoke was beginning to thin. The sound of the wind and the sea came back again. The *Rose* pushed into a clear patch and then she was through.

Lamb blinked his bloodshot eyes rapidly. Directly ahead, towering high into the sky, looking formidably powerful at that range, lay the *Braunschweig*, every detail of her masts, the huge eight-inch gun-turrets, the blue-clad sailors running frantically along her upper deck, painfully clear. Lamb opened his mouth to give his last order.

FIVE

'Not a damn sign of the *Rose* nor the landing party!' Captain Vernon Yorke snapped angrily, as he peered through his glasses at the silent little Norwegian hamlet under the towering snowy cliffs. Ramnes was empty of both Norwegians and British sailors. The one-eyed Captain lowered his glasses and wiped the flying spray from his grey face. 'What the devil do you make of it, Number One? They seem to have damn well vanished into thin air!'

Lieutenant-Commander Jenkins shook his head. 'Sparks has been trying to pick them up ever since you ordered Commander Lamb to take his ship out to escort the convoy in.' He shrugged. 'But he might as well have been trying to contact the moon for all the good it has done him... Do you think, sir, that his receiver might have gone?'

'Impossible!' Yorke barked. 'Those sets could virtually stand up to a direct hit. Under normal circumstances, nothing would knock them out.'

'Hm,' Jenkins said and scratched the back of his neck. 'Well, I'm afraid it's beyond me, sir.'

247

'Not me,' Yorke rasped, ramming his binoculars back in their case angrily. 'You know Lamb and his background, don't you? I wouldn't put anything past a man of that type, especially now that he knows he will be faced with a court martial when the flotilla returns to England.'

Jenkins looked at his Commander aghast. 'But you can't mean that, sir!' he protested. 'Commander Lamb wouldn't ever–'

'Smoke, sir – on the starboard bow,' the young look-out's thick Geordie voice burst into their discussions.

Captain Vernon Yorke was a stickler for accuracy. In spite of his rage and bewilderment at Lamb's mysterious disappearance, he called: 'I've told you before, look-out, that you must try to give an exact bearing … I won't tell you again, my man,' he added severely. Then he took out his glasses and focused them on the starboard bow. Some five miles away, the long stream of dark smoke was painted across the grey-green seascape like the work of an amateur artist who had applied his colour too thickly. He fiddled with the adjustment until the smoke stood out as clear as was possible in the faded light. He gasped. At first he saw a faint pink gleam illuminating the smoke, then he heard the rolling thunder of heavy guns.

He let the glasses drop to his chest. 'Good

grief, Jenkins, did you hear that?'

'I did, sir.' Jenkins swallowed hard. 'Do you think?'

'I do, Jenkins,' Yorke barked, his single eye gleaming. 'The troopers!'

'*One – two – three*,' Doan grunted over each word, as he pressed the electric firing button.

The *Rose* shuddered. One after another, the fish splashed into the water. Running shallow, they headed straight for the stranded cruiser, their lethal course traced by a trail of white bubbles, fanning out, as a delighted Doan had planned that they should, to embrace the whole length of the *Braunschweig*.

The first one missed. Doan groaned aloud as the torpedo ran ashore, its prop whirling harmlessly in the wet sand before it exploded in a cloud of pebbles and dirt. Then the *Braunschweig* shuddered. Doan caught his breath as the second torpedo exploded in a thunderous roar.

'Jesus H Christ,' Doan cried, hardly daring to believe his own eyes, 'we've hit her!'

A second later, as Lamb swung the *Rose* hard to port and sped away for the second attack, the *Braunschweig's* first salvo slammed down only a hundred yards away.

The *Rose*'s torpedo caught the *Braunschweig* squarely amidships. As the noise of the tearing metal drowned even that of the guns, Hass stared at Lutz incredulously. For a long moment, he seemed rooted there, unable to move, unable even to think, his whole being frozen by the shock. Then he shook his head and walked over to the tube of the voice pipe. 'Bridge,' he began. But even as he spoke he heard, as if from another world, the frenzied screams of the trapped engineers, pleading for help. Deathly pale, he snapped the cap on the tube again.

'Lutz, we're stuck.'

'The engines?'

'No. No use even trying. We must stand and fight!'

'Yessir.' Lutz's voice rose in sudden alarm. 'Here the Tommy comes again!'

Beneath them the Oerlikons clattered into life as the turrets swung round, bringing their great guns to bear upon the tiny bucking ship racing towards the *Braunschweig* like a greyhound from hell.

HMS *Rose* skimmed the water, hushing from side to side.

In turret-A Scouse crouched, right eye glued to the rubber eyesight, as the *Braunschweig* loomed, as mighty and as menacing as ever despite the jagged hole in her hull.

250

Down by the torpedo tubes Doan balanced himself as best he could, his thumb poised over the button which would fire the *Rose's* last fish, while Lamb and Degenhardt tensed on the bridge.

As the first harsh crackle of automatic fire split the silence, and white tracer erupted from the cruiser's deck, the air filled with a sharp crackle of exploding 20-mm shells, the hysterical howl of the ricochets and the hollow clang of metal as fist-sized fragments hissed through the shattered rigging to strike the littered deck.

The *Braunschweig's* huge eight-inchers roared. The *Rose* vecred, her superstructure almost touching the water. Lamb grabbed the bridge rail, blinded by the torrent of falling spray, his mouth and lungs full of an acrid smoke. He shook his head and wiped the spray from his face. Behind him the funnel was buckled and hanging to one side like a crushed oil drum. Behind that for ten yards or more the deck had been swept clean by the shell, its grey surface black, three men sprawled out on it in the extravagant attitudes of those who die violently. He staggered to the voice-pipe.

'Bridge – all right in the engine room?' he gasped.

'Och ay, Captain,' the ER9's voice came through, his accent thicker than ever, 'nothin' to greet about!'

251

Behind him two stretcher-bearers were running awkwardly across the littered deck towards the scorched area. They bent and together began to roll the first man over the side.

The *Braunschweig's* guns thundered again. Lamb held on for dear life and un-capped the tube with his free hand. 'Bridge – Doan?'

Doan's voice was strained. In other circumstances, Lamb would not have recognised it. 'Stand by, Doan, to fire torpedoes!' he gasped. 'Another thirty seconds and I'll have to break off attack... Can't take much more of this–'

Below, Scouse opened up with his five-inchers.

'Ay ay, skipper!' Doan yelled.

Faster and faster they flew, the *Braunschweig* growing until she seemed to fill the horizon. Lamb thought he could feel the *Rose's* desperate efforts almost like the beat of his own heart. 'Please God,' he prayed fervently under his breath, 'let me hit her – just one more time!'

They were less than three thousand yards away. The whole starboard side of the *Braunschweig* was alive with the vicious blues and reds of gunfire. It seemed impossible that anyone or anything could survive the tremendous volume of fire.

'Steady now, Coxswain!' Lamb cried

above the roar.

'Steady it is, sir!' Degenhardt yelled back, fighting the wheel, as the *Rose* shivered and shuddered with every fresh blow.

Below Doan tensed. He had come a long way for this moment: the boom of the morning gun at Annapolis; the crisp sound of the cadets' feet on the gravelled walks as they marched to classes; the cocktail parties in the nation's capital and waking up in the morning with a hangover and a new, grateful secretary; the bus ride overnight to Niagara and the grin on the recruiting sergeant's face as he had given his 'Canadian' place-of-birth; the stuffiness and class-consciousness of *King Alfred;* and then unhappy, unlucky *Rose.* He grinned wearily and as he brought his thumb down on the firing button whispered to himself with a sense of finality, 'better than fucking myself to death in Washington, I guess.'

The two-ton fish struck the *Braunschweig* just above her water-line. The explosion blasted inwards and then upwards, running along her suddenly crazy deck sweeping all before it – man and metal – like a huge fireball. The cruiser shuddered convulsively. Panic-stricken men scattered in all directions to get out of the way. Flames shot fifty feet in the air and thick brown smoke began to billow across her crazily tilted deck.

'*Now!*' Lamb cried above the asthmatic

crump of Scouse's guns. *'Hard to starboard!'*

With all his strength, the Petty Officer swung the wheel round, while Lamb gripped the rail and willed her to get safely through the manoeuvre. The last shell of *Braunschweig's* salvo smashed into *Rose's* bow like the blow of a factory hammer. As her bow crumpled into a mass of bent and twisted metal, *Rose* began to lose speed.

Kapitan zur See Hass, capless, blood streaming down one side of his shocked face unheeded, stared at the damage in undisguised horror. But it was not the dead young men sprawled on the battle-littered decks like broken dolls that his eyes saw; it was the *Braunschweig*. The ship, which had seemed impregnable, was a helpless wreck.

'Captain.' It was Lutz, his left trouser-leg gone to reveal a skinny white leg mottled already with the dull lines of varicose veins and the deeper red of the trickle of blood from a wound in his knee. 'We've got...' he swayed and grabbed the bridge rail, 'abandon ship... Fire below... We've got to save ... those we still can...' He wiped a limp hand across his sweat-beaded brow.

'Abandon ship!' Hass exploded. 'You must be crazy, man!'

Savagely he pushed Lutz to one side and crunched across the broken glass which littered the bridge floor. 'Now listen to this,' he barked, flooding the ship with the harsh sound of his voice over the loudspeakers. 'The *Braunschweig* has been grievously hit. But we shall fight on. Our first objective is to rid ourself of that damned destroyer out there before the troopers sail in. Then we will destroy the big fat Tommies, one by one. We owe it to our Folk, our Fatherland, our Führer–' he swallowed hard, his voice suddenly full of emotion – 'our beloved *Braunschweig!*' He pulled himself together again at once. *'Im Namen unseres Führers Adolf Hitler– Sieg heil!'*

As the *Braunschweig's* huge guns – now cranked by hand because of the failure of the electricity supply – swung round slowly to range on the crippled British destroyer only two thousand yards away, a hoarse cry echoed and re-echoed throughout the ship. *'Sieg heil ... sieg heil ... sieg heil...'*

To Hass it sounded like the heady, thrilling music introducing the last act of some Wagnerian tragedy.

The *Rose* lurched. Splintered glass from her shattered lamps scythed through the decks, already littered with dead and dying sailors. Damage control parties raced over the glass to yet another outbreak of fire, as the hail of 20-mm shells stitched a long line of gleaming metal holes along the crippled ship's length. Lamb struggled to his feet once

255

again, blinded with an agonised sweat as his smashed ribs grated against one another.

Machine-gun fire ripped across the bridge. Degenhardt cried out. A stream of blinding blue sparks danced across the instruments. Fresh glass splinters winged their way through the contorted air.

'Are you all right, Coxswain?' Lamb gasped.

'*Verfluchte Scheisse–*' Degenhardt pulled himself together, dropping his native German. 'Yes all right, sir.' He forced his tough, old bleeding face into a leathery smile. 'I always thought the Jerries were better shots than the Tommies, sir,' he joked.

Lamb flashed him a wan smile. 'Right you are, Coxswain. But I want no more proof of their accuracy – thank you.'

'What now, sir? Abandon ship?'

'No. We can't. Those troopers off the fjord over there must have a chance.' He raised his voice above the ever increasing roar. 'The *Rose* will have to stay to face the music.'

'As she has always done.'

Lamb nodded and his pain-racked eyes fell on the seaman lying on his belly just behind A-turret, his bare head pillowed on his arms as if he were asleep. But he was dead – as they all would be before long.

SIX

Captain Yorke's single eye took in the scene at once, as they emerged again from the smoke bank into the grey Arctic twilight: the fat slow troopers steaming closer; the shattered little destroyer wallowing in the troughs, her torn white ensign still flying proudly; while just over a mile away, the crippled hulk of a German cruiser poured broadside after broadside into her.

'It's the *Rose*, Number One,' he barked.

As the sirens howled their hysterical warning and the alarm bells clattered their urgent call to action, he ordered: 'Break out the battle ensign, Number One – we're going in!'

Jenkins flashed the Captain a look and wondered at the almost inhuman coolness with which he faced up to the heavy odds opposing him; Yorke was unnaturally matter-of-fact. No man could be that calm when faced with impending death in its most violent and dreadful form.

'Well, Number One,' he barked, when Jenkins did not move. 'Are you going to get on with it?'

'Ay ay, sir.'

257

As the Number One sped away, Yorke flashed a swift look at the leaden, ominous sky and muttered, 'Lord God of battles, help me and my command to be brave and bold in the conflict to come. Amen.'

The great red, white and blue flag streamed out from below the *Defiance's* yardarm, taut and proud as the wind caught it in its icy grip. Swiftly he jerked the cap off the voice-pipe and snapped: 'Captain here. Engineer, I want every bit of power you've got... Full ahead!'

At thirty-five knots, her forward turrets firing, with shell after shell bursting in brilliant splendour over the enemy cruiser, the *Defiance* surged through the tortured sea past the crippled *Rose,* heading towards inevitable destruction.

Scouse, the blood pouring from his gashed forehead, took his hand from the firing lever and cried: 'Christ almighty, it's the ruddy *Defiance!*'

Doan, lying half-conscious over his torpedo tubes, dreamily spotted her ensign and shaking his head in disbelief, whispered to himself. 'The battle flag ... only old Yorke would do a thing like that!'

And on the *Rose's* shattered bridge, Lamb caught a glimpse of Captain Yorke as the *Defiance* slid by, her deck buried deep in foaming water, her fans roaring mightily as they sucked in air for her oxygen-starved boilers.

In years to come, Lamb's memory of that terrible day would be vague and distorted, but the hazy picture of Yorke with the great ensign streaming out behind him as he sailed to his death would seem to him a kind of symbol, as if the one-eyed Captain could already see more terrible events darkening beyond the *Braunschweig,* and wanted by the manner of his death to pay a token to the already vanishing glory. And then the *Defiance* was past and Lamb knew instinctively that Yorke was going to ram the *Braunschweig,* take her with him as a fitting tribute to the ship and the men he was going to make die with him.

'*Himmel, Arsch und Zwirn!*' Hass cried, his nerve breaking as the new destroyer sped towards him at an incredible speed, her superstructure already in ruins, flames pouring from her stern, but still coming on, 'Can no one stop her?'

At his feet, Lutz lying in a pool of his own blood looked up at him dully and let his head sink wearily. Now to port, frightened sailors were flinging themselves over the rail into the Arctic water, prepared to take their chance thus rather than face the new enemy. But on the starboard side, the 12.7s were still pumping shell after shell at the British destroyer. One thousand metres away, what seemed a solid wall of water thrashed up by the barrage, barred the destroyer's path. But still she came on, emerging from it with a fresh hole torn in her side.

Hass clattered down the ladder from the bridge, stepping over the dead sailors sprawled everywhere. A dying young signaller, his blond hair moving back and forth with the wind, blood trickling from the side of his slack mouth, raised his head and stared at the Captain, his eyes full of pain and a kind of bitter reproach. Hass ran on wildly, trying to forget the look. He pushed by the helmeted sweating, black-faced Number One on the nearest 12.7-cm.

'Hit him, hit him in three devils' name!' he screamed hysterically. 'He's nearly on top of us now!'

Desperately the gunlayer whirled his wheel, smoke-begrimed, bleeding hand clawing the firing lever, his right eye following the wild bucking course of the dying Tommy destroyer. With a grunt, he jerked back the lever.

The shell struck the base of the bridge like the punch of an immense fist. The Captain collapsed against Jenkins's shoulder.

Yorke opened his mouth. He spat blood. 'Let me ... down,' he whispered.

Slowly Jenkins lowered him. 'I'll get the

MO–' he began urgently.

'No time for that now. Promise.'

'Yes, sir?'

'Promise you'll get her!'

The last burst of Tommy pom-pom fire caught Hass as he stood outside the protection of the 12.7's shield. The little explosive shell erupted in his guts, tearing a hole in them, whirling him into a terrible dance of death.

Bone splintered. Blood splattered the deck. His ears were full of his own screams as his helpless body slammed to the metal plates, hot urine streaming down his legs.

'*Mein Führer*,' he gasped, '*mein Führer, ich melde mich ab...*' before death finished his sentence.

The *Defiance* was still doing thirty knots, reeling as the *Braunschweig's* remaining guns struck her, before she slammed into the cruiser. She shuddered as her two thousand tons of driving steel savaged the *Braunschweig's* guts.

For a moment the two ruined ships clung together, screws churning wildly. Then the *Defiance's* A-magazine blew up, blasting off her shattered bow. For a fleeting moment, her stern reared high into the grey sky, propellers spinning madly, her engines still thundering purposelessly. Then she reeled,

261

as if abhorring contact with the enemy ship and plunged to the bottom of the fjord, taking both the quick and the dead with her.

A second later the *Braunschweig's* oil tanks exploded. Two thousand yards away the weary observers felt the shock of that explosion as if a gigantic hand were squeezing their stomachs. A monstrous flaming funeral pyre, the cruiser started to slide into the deeper water. It leapt greedily to receive her, only to recoil, hissing and spluttering angrily as it felt the searing heat of the flames. Then with one final wild tumult of water, she was gone, leaving behind her a shocked silence, and the crippled little ship rocking helplessly in the huge wave which had signalled her end.

EPILOGUE

'Come on, skipper, leg it ... you're gonna miss the war!'

Leading Seaman MacFadden to Lieutenant-Commander Lamb, August 15th 1940.

'Cap'n, yon *Rose* of yours must have more ruddy lives than an alley moggy,' said the shipyard foreman in this thick Geordie accent, and looked up at the grave young Lieutenant-Commander with the first tinges of grey in his dark hair and the bright new ribbon of the DSO next to the DSC on his chest. 'When they towed her in last back-end, she looked to me – if you'll forgive the expression – ripe for the knackers' yard.'

Commander John Lamb grinned and looked at *Rose,* the thick coats of dark grey paint hiding the terrible scars of the Narvik battle. 'Yes,' he agreed, 'new engines, new superstructure and a new B-turret – there's not much left of the old *Rose* except the name, I suppose.'

Up on the *Rose,* he could hear Lieutenant Doan bellowing at Degenhardt, 'get those men moving on deck, Coxswain. We don't want to be still sitting here with our pants down when the Heinies come back. Move it!'

Lamb turned back to the foreman. 'Shall we go over and get that bumf of yours signed, Mr Smithers?'

'Ay sir, that would be a good idea. Jerry'll

be back before dark, mark my words!'

They walked in silence past the Royal Engineers bomb disposal squad, hunched over a 1,000 pounder from the last raid, eyeing with cold dislike the steel monster protruding from the hole they had dug. Smithers quickened his pace. Together they entered the foreman's little office. Nothing had changed except that one wall was decorated with a dirty poster announcing in bold letters: *'THIS IS WHAT YOU MUST DO IF INVASION COMES'*.

The shipyard foreman took off his bowler, hung it on the dusty Victorian hatstand, rubbed his hands on the side of his shiny black jacket, as if to clean them and then produced the release document. For a moment, Lamb allowed his mind to wander, thinking of all the good men who had died since he had last been in this office, how the world had changed and of how old comfortable, self-assured, slow-moving England had gone.

Faintly but definitely the air-raid sirens started to wail further up the estuary. Lamb shook himself out of his reverie. 'Here, Mr Smithers, you'd better let me have that form.'

He scanned through it hastily. 'We Messrs Leslie & Co, Ltd.' he read under his breath, 'Hebburn-on-Tyne at/off the Tyne handed over this fifteenth day of August, 1940 at

4.10 pm o'clock His Majesty's Ship *Rose* to His Majesty's Navy. Received from Messrs Leslie & Co this date without prejudice to outstanding liabilities.'

Further up the river, the first anti-aircraft guns were beginning to open up. The shed's dirty windows started to rattle. The shipyard foreman licked his lips. Lamb understood. Quickly he uncapped his Parker and put his signature beneath the release. 'Here you are, Mr Smithers,' he said and stuck out his right hand. 'And thank you for all your efforts.'

'And thank you, Captain.' Smithers's voice rose slightly as the first menacing throb of aircraft engines came from the east. 'Best of luck,' he said quickly, 'and so long.'

Lamb turned out of the door and a second later was running swiftly across the empty dockyard with the sound of the approaching Heinkels drumming in his ears and Scouse's nasal Liverpudlian voice urging him on from the *Rose's* deck, 'Come on, skipper, leg it … you're gonna miss the war.'